BEING YOUNG CAN BE DANGEROUS

COUGER

When Your Being Haunted

II

A Novel

Billie Dureya Shell

COUGER II

Copyright © 2021

All rights reserved to Billie Dureyea Shell.

Front Cover Image By graphic designer Billie Dureyea Shell & Kenny Writes

First Printing Edition 2021

ISBN 978-1-7373922-2-4

This Book Is Dedicated To All My
Readers

Thank Y'all For All The Love And For
Support As Long As Y'all Keep
Reading I'ma Keep'em
Coming............Y'all Stay Safe And
Remember There's Nothing You
Can't Do If You Put You're Mind To It
And If You Got Mutha fucca's Around
You Saying They Fucc Wit You But
They Telling You Different, Find You
Some New Friends Because Them
Fools Don't Got Yo Best Interest In
Mind. Fuck With People That Believe
In You..... You Will No Who Really
Got Ur Back When Shit Gets Ugiy
Cuz They Will Still Be There!! Now
That's Some Food For Thought...
Enjoy The Book I'm Out..................
Author
Billie Dureyea Shell

ACKNOWLEDGEMENT

First and foremost I have to give honor to My Lord And Saviour Jesus Christ without him now of this would be possible. 2020 was a MUTHA FUCCA Corona Virus made shit hard 4 niggas but we made it threw y'all keep your head up and know that God got us, no matter they throw in our way no one can stop what God has plan for you...

Its 2021 now FUCC 2020 and Covid 19.... Now to my family momma I love you and you no I got you no matter what. You mean the world 2 me oh and NO MORE PINCHING LOL. To my little sister Glenda I love you blackie, you No I Got You always

To my Wife Shatoya Shell you get on my damn nerves 🧍 but I wouldnt trade you 4 anything In the world I love 🖤 you more then words can ever express. To all my children 👶👶 I love y'all Jazmine, Ant'Tuan, Davon, Anthony, David, Lil Dureyea, Alura, Queen Diavion, Cameron, Preniece, Shaniece and Tajh I love u all and I'll 4ever have ur back you all give me a reason 2 smile... to my cousin Zane RIP nigga I miss u more then anyone will ever no, your always remembered love you bro. to my cousin Ty I miss you thank 4 looking out 4 me and Zane you played a big part in my life and I always looked up to you I love you... Uncle Woody I miss you and love you, you no your my favorite uncle... To my nigga Jamal love you, my brothers Lawrence and fred thank 4 showing me the game I love yall 4 that. To my oldest sister Nedra love you thank you 4 always having my back. to my family uncles anties cousins etc.. I love y'all even those of you that act funny as fuck

To my dark side niggas y'all no what it is YAAH GANG....
Now to all my readers and fans I love you thanks for reading I
hope u enjoy this book as much as I enjoy writing
them with this Corona Virus 19 shit there ain't shit to do but
write so I'm on my shit with that being said y'all be safe cover
your face and love each other life is short so love the ones that
really love I'm gone no. enjoy the book

STAY SAFE

Author Billie Dureyea Shell

THERE'S NOTHING U CANNOT DO
IF U PUT UR MIND 2 IT.

All you nigga's got EDD money so aint no excuse
why you can't get a book LOL

CHAPTER 1

A bitch was chillaxin'. I'd stopped by Ty's last night and as soon as I unlocked my front door, Jarvis was rollin' up. Got damn! Tha pretty, popular and sexy are always in demand, that be me bitches! Not really in tha mood, 'cause Ty wore a sista out, I gave him a call, lied and said I had cramps, then screamed in horror. "Oh hell naw!" Somebody had come in my shit and tossed blue paint all ova my damn furniture! Eyes wide in disbelief, I stepped back out, peeped who was outside, then walked inside. "Ooo I'ma kick some tail today and whoever did dis grimy shit better have some dough cause they're gonna pay for all new shit. Believe dat!" * Daylight hit and I was outside wearin' jeans, a tee and tightly laced timbs. No Vaseline required, cause I neva ever let a jealous hoe get close enough to scratch me. No way you gone have me lookin' an ugly mess, I'm just sayin'. Seemed like everyone and they momma was outside,

9

like they knew shit was 'bout to pop off. And it was. The Courts held a lotta hatin' hoes which ain't stop jack ova here, cause I'ma fuck who I want, go where I want and say what I want. I'm just sayin'. Spottin' Kelly and dis chick named Mavis, I stomped over, adrenaline pumpin'; ready to take it to dis fake hoe once and for all. Soon as I get close, I peep tha sneaky look on her face. My eyes drop and there it was; blue paint under nails and a few splatters on knuckles. I o'nt know why dese youngins' get to smellin' they self and wanna come for moi, but her ass gone learn today that Taylor James don't play with kids. I get their asses sucked out at the abortion clinic, slurpp! I'm just sayin'. Runnin' up, I punched Kelly dead in tha eye, her ass yelped like a scalded cat. My knuckles throbbed 'cause I threw all my weight behind it. Mavis threw her hands up and backed away. 'That's right boo, you don't want none of dis ass whoopin' I'm deliverin'.' Kelly swung back all wild, tha shit flew ova my shoulder. Maybe she couldn't see cause dat eye was closin' faster than a hoe spread her legs for a trick. "Stupid ass!" I yelled, followed by a knee to the gut. "Yo dumb ass still got blue paint on yo hands!" Another to the chin, which knocked her ass from folded over to standin'. Kelly swung again, missed and grabbed my ponytail. Too bad its detachable boo. That shit came right off, leavin' her with a silly ass look on her face; so I hit her with a four piece just for lookin' like dat. Blood shot out of her nose and mouth, splatterin' my tee. Her ass lucky tha shirt wasn't a favorite or I'd really take it to Kelly's ass. "Taylor! Get off my daughter!" blared in my ears. Rosalie grabbed my arm mid swing usin' my momentum to turn me in her direction. "What are you doin'!? She's a child Taylor! If you've got a problem with mines, bring it to me!" bossed Rosalie; standin' before me in shorts, bra and half a head of braids. Kelly lay moanin', bleedin' at my feet. "Yo bitch ass daughter broke in my shit and poured blue paint ova my furniture; and before you tune up them lyin' ass lips, the evidence is all under her fuckin' nails. Now I don't give two shits how ya'll do it, but my shit better be replaced by the end of the day; cause if you think this bad, just wait." I barked back, then chest bumped her ass. "Whatchu not gone do is stand in my face and threaten mines Taylor. You might pump fear in people out here, but I'm not one." Shocked, I gave Rosalie another look. "Really? Well take dis bit of knowledge so you'll know I'm serious." I said, then kicked her in her pus', socked her in the nose and walked off wit a dust of hands. * Three hours later, I'm sittin' at the kitchen table munchin' on pizza bites when I hear a buncha yellin' and what not. Peekin' out tha window, I see Toni all up in Mavis' face. "Aww shit, round two." I swear these hoes love to keep shit goin'. I'm just sayin'. Slidin' on flip flops, I stepped outside into chaos. A big ass fight was in progress! Weave, someone's wig and extended lashes lay scattered. People were yellin' and some dude jumped in after one girl hit tha ground and lay motionless. Shirts were ripped off puttin' stretchmarks, burn marks, cuts and keloids on display. Blood, slob and a few teeth flew; raggedy bras and holey drawers came into play when two girls were beat out there clothing. Mavis yanked Caren's bra up and over her head, dudes made gaggin' noises at the sight of flapjacks she called tits. 'Ump, dis girl only seventeen and had no kids, so why yo shits lookin' like elephant tits? Shit so saggy she could step on her own titty. One was way bigger than the otha, while the smaller oozed a pus like substance. Another chick had a navel ring; the ring had rust and green shit growin' outta it and was turnin' her outtie navel rainbow colors. Sirens could be heard quickly approachin'. I saw Dove roll up, so side steppin' tha ruckus, I strode over and jumped in the car. Dove grabbed a box of Raisinets and started munchin' away while Bryson Tiller played on the radio. "Gurll what tha fuck jumped off WWF's Royal Rumble outchere?" Dove asked, eyes all wide. Dis nosy trick always in somebody's business, just messy. "Not sure. It started between Toni and Mavis." I shrugged, cause all I cared about was seein' a furniture truck roll up wit' my shit. Cops jumped out, yellin' 'cease and desist', which was ignored until they pulled out expandable batons and started wackin' knees and crackin arms until order was somewhat restored. "Wow, Sincere jus' took off. They aren't catchin' dat mafucka." joked Dove. "Right. Anyhoo it's Thursday, wanna hit up tha Legion or the Elks?" Dove twisted her lips. "I guess so, ain't like no other clubs jumpin' on a Thursday." "A'ight." I opened the door and got out. "Come scoop me around eleven." Dove frowned. "Eleven? You know clubs close early tonight, we need to be there before that. Shit, I'm tryina leave saucy. You know them old bastards shell out the cash." "Fine, ten and not a minute earlier." Slammin' the door, I saw Toni stridin' in my direction. I hope her ass don't try and do me 'cause she sees a few cops out dis piece; cause I'll still pound her shit to tha white meat and happily skip my black ass to the cruiser. "Uh, Taylor.. can I speak to you for a sec?" Eyebrow arched, I gave the screw face cause whatchu got to say to moi? That I beat cho mom and sister's ass and now you want some too? Or is it you got my money? Or furniture receipt? "What?" Toni pulled a slip of paper out her bra and passed it. I took that shit with two fingers. Did I smell musk? Ooo, dats tha worse when you got breast musk, I'm just sayin'. It was an invoice from Raymour & Flanigan for a couch, loveseat, recliner and table. My eyes slid down to the total, $3500. A smile formed. "Thanks, and when can I expect my furniture?" "Tomorrow afternoon." My smile grew. "Thank Brick for me." Turning, I made my way inside, then called Jacko to come toss this crap for forty bucks. * "Damn, I forgot to tell Tay' 'bout me beatin' up Aisha last night." Dove muttered aloud, wide smile gracing her lips. Hearing the house phone ringing Dove quickly stepped inside and snatched it up. "Hello?" "Bitch! When I see yo ass it's a wrap! You put Aisha in the hospital, she lost my son!" Roared Bernard, harsh breathing assaulting her ear. "Who's this?" Teased Dove, pulling out her last bogie. she lit up deeply inhaled then rolled her eyes. "Fuck you Dove.." "Besides," she cut in. "...you've already got a son, he's at yo moms. Why don't you go see his ass insteada worryin' 'bout a dead fetus; and for tha record, that trick stepped to me and got what her hand called for, a mothafuckin' beat down!" Dove yelled back. she could hear Bernard's teeth grinding. "Yeah, I'll see you shorty and getcho bastard from my momma's!" "What!? Nigga you lunchin', dats his G'ma.." "Hoe please." Bernard said cutting her short. "Dat DNA test I took came back. My momma called me and told me I'm 99.999% not Jeff's father. So hop yo sorry, dick ridin', non cleanin' ass, STD walkin' self to my momma's before I leave dis hospital and set his lil ass on da curb. No more babysitter bitch!" Click. Stunned, Dove stared at the phone in disbelief. Yeah Jeff wasn't his, but never in a million years did she think Bernard would develop the smarts to check on his own. * Dressed casually in Dereon jeans and top and Roman sandals, I jumped in Dove's car and did a double take. Jeff waved hello then said, "Where you hoes goin' tonight?" Woosa Tay' don't climb ova tha seat and serve his lil grown ass.

"Nigglet dats none of yo b.i. I'ma grown ass woman.." "I know," Jeff licked ashy lips, "and I can't wait to tap dat cause yo man ain't hittin' you right. You too up tight." My jaw dropped, Dove pulled off like she don't hear her man-child comin' at me sideways. Now when I slap his ass off da seat she bet not say shit then either. "Jeff, how old are you?" He smirked. "Old enough. My momma say you like 'em young anyway, so why you playin' shorty?" My head whipped in Dove's direction. Dis trick gone turn up her staticky ass radio. "A'ight, I'll let you have dat Jeff." "Hmp, what else you gone let me have?" He stuck his tongue out and flapped it back and forth. Ooo, dis lil ninja was really tryina take me there! I could feel the switch itchin' to flip. Thankfully Dove pulled over on Tower Avenue, put the car in park and jumped out. "C'mon boy, I don't got all night." she griped. "Who lives here?" I asked, clueless on why we'd stopped before a peach single family house. "Brian and his girl Tiphanie." Slammin' the door, Dove marched up the driveway, Jeff and two suitcases in tow. Before she could knock, the door swung open and there stood Brian. He hadn't changed much. I could see him strainin' to get a good look at who sat in tha front seat and since I wanted no parts, I turned my back, whipped out my cell and jumped on Facebook. Flippin' through some pics, my lips twisted. Ump, some hoes have no damn shame, postin' all their business. Postin' there man's dick size, postin' pics of them in bra and panties; tha shit went on and on. Take an ad out and sell tha pus' why don't you. Mavis had posted a video of the fight which I shared on my page. Shit, next time I gotta kung fu a hoe I'mma have someone film it so I can post it on Girl Fights, Gorilla Fights, Mediatakeout and Bossip; cause dese bitches getting' beside they self and need to be reminded who tha hell I be. I'm just sayin'. Brian started yellin' so I cracked tha window to get my listen on. "Look Brian, I could give a lion's stankin' pussy on how Tiphanie's gonna feel when she comes home from suckin' d..I mean work. Jeff's yo son and its time he gets to know you! Now either we do this or I'll see yo ass in child support court. Plus, I'll tell everybody how dat trick done brainwashed you and turned you against yo own flesh and blood." She lashed. Brian gasped like a fish outta water for a hot second, before he fully opened the door, allowin' Jeff in and takin' his luggage. Dove strutted down the drive like she was America's Next Top Model. Please, more like America's Top Slut, or the next hoe who thinks her pus' is tha ultimate smorgasbord. I'm just sayin'...

CHAPTER 2

Dove drove past the American Legion which had about ten cars, then decided to see how the Elks fared. They were packed! The parking lot and both sides of a oneway were fulla cars. "Aww sukey! Hurry up, I see a car leavin' tha lot!" Dove's non drivin' ass rolled up on the curb, cut cross the grass and damn near blocked the Honda leavin' the exit. At the door they were chargin' eight which surprisingly Dove paid for she and I. Inside, every table was full, along with the stools at the bar. People leaned against walls and crowded the dance floor. "Good evening ladies, may I buy you drinks?" Issey Miyake surrounded me. Smilin', I turned and came face to face with dis he-she named Reba. I mean ole gurl had her boobs lopped off and took hormone pills and injections. If you didn't know her before alla this, you'd never know she was a girl until she dropped her boxers. Reba aka Ron was a better lookin' dude. I'm just sayin'. "Hey Ron." purred Dove with a hug so tight her boobs were smooshed. Ump, some people have no shame I tell ya. I think Dove's ass would fuck a horse if the price was right. Chuckle. "Hey Dove. Taylor, long time no see." Since Dove wanted the floor, I let her have it. I excused myself and hit up the bar, head bobbin' to the sounds of my bitch Lil Kim. That's my mafuckin' dog right there. I saw her years ago in concert and ever since can't nobody say shit 'bout her while I'm around. YoYo's crazy ass was runnin' tha bar. For a time, she and I were tight; 'til ha dick drove her crazy and she ended up hittin' her ex's new girl with her car, then backed up and ran her over. Ump, dat must've been some good damn dick to make a chick try and kill another with her rental car. That's a lil to much, even for moi. "Aww do the stanky leg! My homie Taylor in da house!" Screamed YoYo the other bartender, jumped and dropped a Heinken on the floor in surprise. "Hey YoYo, how's it goin'? Where you been hidin'?" "Prison. Just got out last year an shit, tryin' to get the twins back. Sup wit' you?" I shrugged. "Same shit, different tissue. Let me get a Sex on the beach. Nah, let me get a Snakebite." YoYo wiggled her bushy brows. "Girl, member when we'd drink dem shits, den hit tha club? Whoo those was some good times!" "Damn! Can you stop reminiscing and make my damn drank!? You wanna flashback, flashback on all da pus' you ate and mop handles up yo snatch, fuck outta here! Reminisce on how yo ass got ten years wit' a mandatory eight and two of probation."

"Yeah, those were the days alright." YoYo finally passed me my shit, told me it was on the house, winked, licked her lips and served the next waitin' customer; givin' me a chance to fully take her in. Once slim, YoYo was damn near as wide as a deep freezer. Where she wouldn't be caught dead without make-up and fresh hairdo, her face was plain, not even lip gloss adorned crunchy lips; and she'd cut off full, shoulder length locks and now sported a small afro. See what a dick a do to you. Weak bitches, I swear. The DJ threw on another oldie, Blaque's 808 and the dance floor swelled with couples. I could see Dove and Reba cuttin' a rug, that's right, I said Reba. She ain't no damn Ron if a penis ain't swingin' between her legs to prove it. "Wanna dance?" Hot ass, liquored breath fried my nape hairs. 'Fuck, I ain't in the mood for no b.s.' Turnin', face all twisted, I glared at dude before me. High yellow, face full of freckles, a big wide nose and large booty eatin' lips. 'Lips so big he smiles and wets his hair. Lips so big he needs a paintbrush to swipe on Chapstick.' I'm just sayin'. "No thanks, I'm jus' chillin'." I started to say maybe lata, but why lie; I wasn't dancin' wit' dude now or later, somethin' 'bout his ass rubbed me tha wrong damn way. Kinda like when you rub yo pet so hard they snap at cho ass. Openin' my purse, I pulled out a cigarette and a pair of brass knuckles. As I've said before, yo girl stays ready fo' da bullshit. "What? Hoe don't get beside yo'self, it's just a dance. You ain't all dat!" Spittle

19

flew, landin' on my hand. Nasty bastard; the switch jiggled. "Uh hunh, well then gone 'bout yours and ask someone else to dance." Dude weaved on his feet while his eyes rolled like he had no control over their muscles. "Don't..you..hoe I said let's dance, or you gone have problems!" Suddenly he grabbed my arm hard while pullin' me off the stool. I knocked over my Snakebite. "Nucca, dat liquor done made you fuck wit' tha right one!" I blasted and came up swingin'. he stumbled from the blow while blood dribbled under his right eye. Dats right, the switch was all the way up, so far dat mafucka was stuck. Dude roared like a wounded grizzly, raised a hand and cupped bloody face. "You. You h..hit me." he slurred. Being that it was so packed, security couldn't see what had popped off, so I jabbed his shocked ass twice more before some chick saw what was goin' on and started chantin'; "Security, security to the dance floor!" Dove came runnin' behind security, took one look at dude on the floor rollin' and moanin' like he took a bullet to the gut and burst out laughing. "Tay' why you beatin' up Guy? Yo ass crazy!" She bellowed. Hands on hips, I glared between the two. "Guy? Who the fuck is Guy!?" Dove giggled. "Dats Marcus' step daddy girl. He saw me on tha dance floor, asked if I wanted a drink. I tol' him hell yeah and to buy my girl Tay one too." She looked down, watching the two bouncers help Guy up. "Jeez his cheekbones swellin' somethin' serious, you might've broke his joint." Shrug.

'Cause I don't car either way. Plus, tha drunk bastard didn't ask if I wanted a drink, he got all up in my space actin' all ignant, so he got what his hand called for. "Whateva." Lip smack. "Guy spilled my shit. You sent dat drunk fool ova here, so dig in dat grungy bra, pull out sum green and get me anotha." I ordered. 'Was dis chick fo' real?' thought Dove. 'How am I responsible cause she wildin' out? Suddenly I really want dis hoe to suffer.' Pulling a wrinkled twenty from bra, Dove squeezed in at the bar, flagged down some butch lookin' chick and ordered herself a Rum Punch and Tay's Snakebite, Dove had half a mind to accidently on purpose knock said drink dead in her lap. "Here you lush." Taylor snatched her drink then smirked. "So where's yo boyfriend? Y'all were all hugged up and swappin' spit." Dove chuckled. "Oh, you saw that hunh?" "Hmm, what's up with you Dove? One minute you on dick and tha next you bumpin' twats?" Dove sipped her drink, winked and walked off. *

CHAPTER 3

"**Y**o Dove, hol' up!" Just about to jump in her car to go check on Jeff, she was halted by Kione's fione self. Sultry smile in place, Dove closed the door, then leaned against it. "Hey stranger. Where you been hiding witcho cute self?" Kione walked up so close their knees collided. Dove's eyes widened in surprise at the move. "I had some shit to take care of but I'm back now. So what's up ma?" 'Wait...what? Did I hear that shit right?' Dove silently questioned, ready to take it as far as Kione was willing to go. 'Fuck, I wanted him first.' her thoughts continued. "Wateva, you want to be is up." Kione smiled and leaned in for a quick smooch. 'Damn, his ass tastes like melted chocolate.' she ruminated. "Why don't we hook up later at my place?" Dove asked. Kione cupped her breast and ran a thumb over distended nipple. "Yo joint harder than stone, got a nigga mouthwatering and shit." "Oh yeah? Well I can definitely help you with that." She purred, pussy juicing from nipple stimulation. "What time you wanna see dis big dick?" Mouth drying, Dove wiggled a lil bit and felt nothin' but heat and hardness pressed against her. Pictures of Kione's dick in her mouth, her tongue up firm cheeks, had her knees trembling. 'Wait..what had he asked her? Oh yeah, what time.' Mused Dove. "Um, midnight." Kione smiled. "A'ight, midnight it is. Be ready fo' a hella workout." Kione tweaked her nipple, forcing a moan from parted panting lips. "See you lata shorty." Dove watched him depart, thoughts of riding what felt like ten inches stewing, only for Taylor to impede her thoughts. 'Hmm, how would Taylor feel once she found out Kione's dick held her pussy juices?'Another thought slid in. What if she caught them in the act? After all, Taylor had done her wrong on numerous occasions. She always had some slick shit to say and she'd had her kidnapped for her own sick ass reasons; so a lil payback was definitely in order. Pleased smirk on her face, Dove opened the car door and jumped in. * "Bitch! I'm here to check on my son! Not to stand here debatin' wit' yo ugly insecure ass!" barked Dove. For the past ten minutes she'd stood ringing Brian's doorbell, only for the curtains to flutter. So Dove kept her finger on the bell until Tiphanie finally yanked it open with a dumb look plastered on her face. "Where's Jeff?" demanded Dove, eyes trying to see around Tiphanie's wide frame. "I don't appreciate

you popping up at my home, that's what phones are for.."
"Listen fatty," Dove cut in. "I give zero fucks about how you
feel. I came to check on mines, so go get his ass or get out the
damn way!" She barked again. Tiphanie, who felt self-conscious
about her weight, flushed a deep red at the insult. "I beg your
pardon? How dare you! So what I'm a little overweight. Brian
doesn't complain when I ride him, so take your bony, insult
having ass away from my home this instant!" Tiphanie screamed
back, breathing erratic. She tried to calm down before an asthma
attack had her visiting the E.R. again. Dove laughed. "Yo half
breed ass don't even know how to cuss." she chuckled again.
"And fo' tha record Hefty cinch sack, I'm totally grossed out
from the thought of yo ass ridin' anythin'; especially Brian's sexy
ass." Tiphanie's eyes watered, seein' it Dove went in for the kill.
"Hmp." she smacked her lips like she'd just finished a four piece
from Kfc. "I can still remember suckin' dat dick. Does he still
shiver when you stick yo tongue in tha slit? Does he still like
doggy style the best?" Dove moaned. "and the way dat mafucka
eats da pus' should be against tha law. Anyway, I've taken up
enough of your time. I don't see Brian's car, so I'll stop by the
barber shop. Ta ta." sang Dove, as she turned and strode back to
her car. * Shop Rite was packed and it wasn't even check day.
Normally I shopped at Stop N Shop, but because I had a buy
one, get one free coupon for a bag of whiting for Shop Rite, I

took a drive out to Wethersfield; which was the closest. I'd invited Joshua over for dinner tomorrow and with nothing in my freezer, so to the store I went. Grabbing a cart, I started over by the lettuce and tomatoes, ignoring hateful glares from a few white people. As long as they stayed in their lane, the switch wouldn't flip on they ass. I'm just saying. Pickin' up a pack of ribs, I felt someone starin' hard as fuck. Refusin' to look around, I left the meats and went up the cereal aisle; yo gurl loved some Honeycomb cereal. Pickin' up two boxes, I hit the next aisle and hear, "Taylor! What a coincidence seeing you here. I've called and texted you numerous times, but you never answered. Did your number change or something?" I knew dat irritating ass voice anywhere. Glancing up, there he was, ole Brandon from the club. He wore boat shoes and Bermuda shorts with a tee that read, 'Single looking to mingle!' Corny ass. With a huff, I gave a dry ass, "Sup." and started to push my cart when dis ninja grabbed it. "You were right. About going black and never going back. I miss you Taylor. I hope you feel the same now that fate's brought us together." Was dis fool for real? Was I bein' punked? Crazy shone brightly from his eyes, like a beacon on a stormy night. The switch jiggled. "Dats nice and all, but I'm busy. See you around." I told him. Not if I could help it. I swear, you fuck a mafucka one time and they think they own yo ass; crazy stalkin' bastard. Brandon reached out and grabbed my arm. Oh no he didn't! Switch on, I let him have a slice of get right. "First off, don't touch me unless fuckin' invited!" I snapped all loud. A few custies in the aisle gave a look, while a Hispanic girl pulled out her cell and started recording. "Second, buy a clue. If I don't answer yo calls and texts, that means kick rocks, I ain't interested. Now unless you got two g's in yo pocket, ain't shit else to discuss!" A hurt look slid over his face like tha shit was supposed to fuckin' faze me. Please, money talks and bullshit runs a marathon. I'm just sayin'. Before I could really go ham, some heavyset florid faced white man with a badge that read, manager Oscar Martin, hurried towards us. "Sir, is this young lady harassing you? It was brought to my attention there was a disturbance." He turned watery green eyes on me. "Young lady, here at Shop Rite we do not condone harassment or solicitation of our customers of any type." he faced Brandon. "Sir if you'd like, I can detain her while I call the police." See. His ass threatenin' a bitch with the law. Hunny chile call dem sons of bitches, cause Taylor James always has bond money okay! "Listen you fat, sweaty faced, racist bastard. If yo ass put down the snack long enough to have checked tha security tapes before speed walkin' ova here accusin' me of bullshit, you would've saw me mindin' mines and dis asshole followin' and harassin' me. So call tha fuckin' po-po and when they get here and I raise so much hell they'll have no choice but to view 'em, then release me, I'll call every news channel and a damn good lawyer to sue you and dis fuckin' store!" Oscar glanced at Brandon, only to find he no longer stood there; his hand held green basket the only proof that he'd been there at all. "Um, I..I'm so sorry for the misunderstanding Ms.?" I kept quiet, switch all tha way turnt the hell up. "Yes..well," he cleared his throat. "There's no need to take things that far ma'am. I'm sure we can come to some sort of arrangement." My brows arched. "I'm listenin'." "How about a one-hundred-dollar gift card?" He pleaded. With holdin' a grin, I pretended to ponder over Oscar's words. "Uhm, I don't know. I've never been so embarrassed...." "Three hundred." Oscar hastily threw out. I glanced at my cart two boxes of cereal and a pack of ribs. "Throw in my groceries and we have a deal." "Done." Needless to say, I walked outta Shop Rite with three-hundred-dollar gift card and four hundred and seventy five dollars' worth of free groceries. *

CHAPTER 4

"You comin' thru or nah?" Dove smartly asked while snappin' and poppin' gum. I stared at the phone. 'Ooo, dis trick tryina do me. Lord I ask dat you lay hands on dis hoe before I do; 'cause I'll lump her shit up with da very receiver she's tryin' me on. Amen. "I o'nt know girl, yo place looks like you got tha city dump in yo place. Yo ass got so many pets runnin' round, you done named dem mafuckas Ronnie, Bobby, Ricky and Mike; and when you sit down to eat, bam! There's Johnny crawlin' cross ya plate." Pow! How ya like me now bitch? I done told these chicks don't come fo' moi; cause you ain't ready fo' tha burn the pain my words and dese fists deliver. I'm just sayin'. Pregnant pause. Aww, did I hurt ya feelin's' I silently think in a voice used for baby talk. "Ah ha ha I didn't know Kevin Hart was yo brotha. You crack me up....not! Now ain't nobody beggin' or kissin' yo ass; just a simple yea or nah okay. 'Cause I ain't beat fo' all yo extras." snapped Dove.

"Okay, what time?" I asked, cause already I'm done wit' dis phone call. Joshua and tomorrows dinner was on my mind, not dis wack ass get togetha Dove had slapped together. "Good. Eleven, eleven thirty. See you lata." Dove hung up, "Weak hoes always get in they feelins'. Dove know her shit was nasty, so me callin' her on it shouldn't touch a nerve; and if it did, den clean tha fuck up. And she wonderin' why her ass can't keep a damn man." I said aloud. Her and her apartment needs a complete overhaul. I'm just sayin'. * Heart racing, Dove snatched a bottle of bacon bits and a pouch of dried cranberries with walnuts, then slammed the cabinet closed and finished preparing dinner; then jumped in the shower. Dressed in a cute lavender sleeveless mini dress, Dove sprayed on a little Amber from Victoria's Secret, slid her feet into flats and smiled from a knock on the door. Show time! Anita Baker sang on BET as Dove opened the door. "Hey gurlie." sang Glenda who passed over a six pack of strawberry wine coolers; followed by Rosalie and her two daughters, with Taylor bringing up the rear. "Hey ya'll. Thanks for comin', have a seat. Anybody want a drink?" Dove asked, being nice and playing hostess while smirkin' at the sight of Tay's face all twisted up. I snorted, and followed Dove's ole sneaky butt into the kitchen. "I thought this was a get together?" "It is." I eyed dis trick. A get together hunh? Then why her ass dressed for tha club? And what in tha land of holey drawers is

Toni, Kelly and Rosalie doin' here? See, if we gone be on some funny shit, let me invite my cousin China over and see how tha wind blows. "Need some help?" Dove jumped. Uh ah, why yo ass all skittish? Yo ass up to somethin'. "Uh..sure. Grab those plastic cups and the Patron and Paulie for me." I grabbed it and walked back into the living room. The four were in a heated debate about the group Jodeci, who were singin' 'Come and talk to me.' "Girl is you blind?" barked Rosalie, as she lit Black & Mild in hand. "Devante's ass is sexy as hell. He so sexy, I'd munch on musty balls and gargle the sweat between his toes." Toni burst out laughing, spewin' the mouthful of sunflower seeds she sucked on all over the coffee table. "Please." snorted Kelly. "Have you seen him lately? They all look fresh outta rehab for every drug invented. They're so over tha hill you can't see they asses." I burst out laughin', she had a point. I saw KC and his brother's video before they reformed Jodeci, and dudes jaw was grindin' and swingin' all ova tha place. The other looked like he had Parkinson's. I'm just sayin'. Settin' down bottles and cups, I copped a squat next to Glenda on the loveseat, prayin' I didn't regret it later with a slew of roach bites on my hips and back. Talk and laughter flowed easily until Ms. Let Me Start Shit took it there. "Before we eat, I just wanna thank everyone for coming over. I know we've all had issues with each other, so I wanted to clear the air. We're all grown here and should be able to do so without a bunch of he say, she say throwin' around." Ohh, Dr. Phil has arrived. How 'bout you analyze why you wanna be me, or how 'bout why yo shitty ass apartment always smells like chopped cat on a hot plate? Or how 'bout why you jump on and ride sloppy seconds? Ump, I can go on and on all night, cause dis tricks just ri-got-dam-diclous. I'm just sayin'. Glenda raised her hand, cleared her throat and asked, "How come you lied on me Dove? I thought we were cool, but your lies ended up puttin' me in the hospital." Ooo, yass Glenda! Serve her ass a heapin' portion! "You're right and I apologize." Wait..say what now? "I guess I was jealous." continued Dove, lookin' all contrite. Trick please, you can fool some of dese blind hoes, but Taylor Janae sees through yo fake exterior okay. "Okay apology accepted, but I still wanna know why?" Glenda repeated. Dove took a deep breath, then started this cock and bull spiel that I tuned out, cause if you wanna believe Dove's lies, who am I to tell her nay. Next thing I know, the two are cryin' like Oprah had reunited long lost mother and daughter; ugh gag me. Toni and Kelly eyed me. "Why do you keep so much drama goin' wit' us?" Really? Duh, 'cause I don't like you hot body bitches. Ya nasty, ya triflin', ya ghetto as fuck and you stomped yo sista til' she miscarried, how 'bout dat. Instead I answered with, "Because my issue was with Rosalie who's grown, but you both felt some type and brought it to me." Kelly rolled her eyes, while Toni snorted,

"You started shit first when you told my sister 'bout Brick and I." Said Toni; foot tappin' like she was seconds away from pouncin'. "Sure did and?" Was my answer, ain't no shame in my game hunny. If I say or do, best believe I own mines; whereas these two mangy cats in heat keep tip toeing around the real issue, that they both want Brick for themselves. They played the nice wit' each other role, while behind closed doors, Toni was goin' balls out to get Brick to choose her. Like I've said before, don't do me boo, 'cause you won't like tha outcome. "Well we wanna know why? Why do you care who's sexin' Brick? Jealous much?" added Kelly. I made myself a glass of Paul while Dove sat up a foldin' table and started bringin' out bowls of salad and bread. "Nah sweetie, you got tha wrong one on that jealousy tip. You need to look to tha left, 'cause I don't want Brick's hoe ass and trust; I'm never jealous." Toni and Kelly's necks snapped to their left and came face to face with Dove's back. Both girls jaw dropped. "Wait." I said just as Dove moved to reenter the kitchen revealing Rosalie who sat at the table buttering a dinner roll. Bam! How you like me now. "Wait, are you accusin' our mother of sexin' Brick behind our backs?" Smirk. Rosalie froze mid bite. "Ask her." I said. Both girls stood and joined her at the table. Dove entered carryin' a big bowl of spaghetti and another filled with sauce and meatballs. Standing, Glenda and I followed suit. "Everyone dig in. I hope you all enjoy." she said, picked up tongs and pulled out spaghetti noodles. "Ma, don't sit here actin' like you ain't just hear what Taylor said. Is it true? Have you been messin' wit' Brick behind our backs?" They both threw out, eyes and mouth wide in anticipation. Rosalie looked around the room, down at her plate and took a deep breath. "Taylor's right." gasps rang out. "I've been messin' around wit' Brick way before either of you met him. He was young so we kept it secret, meetin' up while you girls were in school. When tha drug business got good, we'd meet up in hotels or go away on day trips. Then Kelly started talkin' 'bout her new man Brick. I didn't want to steal her happiness, so Brick and I agreed to keep what we'd done between us; while he determined which of us or none of us he wanted." Well damn! Its truth or consequences up in here? Holla! Toni's ole weak behind burst into tears, jumped up over turnin' her chair and ran outside. Munchin' on a roll, I must admit I was actually enjoyin' this lil get togetha of Dove's; until Glenda screamed. This chick had scooped up a mafuckin' mouse tail! Rosalie gagged, then released vomit all over the table and her lap. Kelly glanced inside the sauce bowl, shuddered, then eyed the salad. A daddy long legs was crawlin' out tha fuckin' salad bowl! Pushin' from the table, all I could think was, Damn, I'm glad I ain't eat nothin'. Walkin' to tha door, I gave tha barf face one last glance, yanked open the door and ran smack into Kione. My son. The fucka knew who I was and made it his mission to have sex with me. Bastard. "Ma." No surprise in his voice, so I knew off tha bat Dove had done this crap. With a salty smirk, I pushed his ass out tha way, and strutted down the sidewalk.

CHAPTER 5

Ump, that damn dinner was a fuckin' horrible mess chile, just horrible. From tha rat tail spaghetti sauce, to the spider salad and the Oprah like intervention. Chucklin'. I lit up a cigarette, inhaled deeply, then sighed. Tonight Joshua was comin' for dinner. I didn't mind cookin' or invitin' him over, it was tha fact dude was white, rollin' up in tha hood in a nice ride. These nosy ninjas ain't miss jack and would assume an undercover was at my place. Was I snitchin'? Was I wearin' a listenin' device? A camera? These questions could cause major problems for me, so scoopin' up my cell I dialed his number; got his voice mail and left a message explainin' that dinner was still on, just at his place or to a restaurant. I apologized for tha last minute switcheroo and told him to call me. That out the way, thoughts of Dove returned. I remember when I first met her ass... It was the last night of Jamaican week and I'd decided to attend the parade durin' the day, go to the cuisine fair in the evenin' and hit up a couple clubs that night. For the parade I threw on some white short shorts, left the flap open so my pink studded thong was on display and a halter top that stopped right above my navel. Sliding into white fresh out the box Nike Uptowns, I'd had my hair done in micro block braids, grabbed my purse and was out. The parade was off tha chain! Men were everywhere! Tall, with bald domes that glistened under beaming sun, men who were shirtless, showing off buff upper bodies, men in basketball shorts, dick print proudly on display. Ump, ump! it was like an all you can eat buffet, where you wanted everything but didn't know where to start first. People were crowding the streets, cheering, drinkin', just having a good damn time, when I spotted Dove's ass. Of course, at the time I didn't know that. Anyway, ole girl wore a white fishnet one piece with red bra and thong underneath; and flip flops on her feet. One of the male performers pulled her close, to the sounds of Buju Banton. Then later that evening, I saw her at the cuisine fair. She'd slid on cutoff jeans over the fishnet and had a wife beater slung around her neck. Bitches were hatin' as she strutted through. I'm like don't hate, step yo game up boo, then maybe someone will give yo dusty ass a second look. I'm just sayin'. Later that night, I changed into jeans and bikini top; and club hopped until I saw the West Indian was poppin'! Dem bastards wanted forty at the door, which included free drinks for the ladies; which saved they're asses a cursin' out like none other. Forty dollars! Are you servin' Mignon and lobster up in dis piece? No, well fuck outta here witcho forty dollars to get in bullshit. Because there were some fione specimens walkin' around and they outnumbered the women, I happily paid and stepped inside to Tanya Stephens. I hit up the bar, turnin' down 'let me buy you a drank' pick up lines. Really Sir Wacks A Lot, women drink free tonight; fuck outta here! An eye roll and my back was all they got. Drink in hand. I walked around, scopin' out my dick for the night. When Elephant Man's 'Signal Da Plane' came on, I ain't neva seen tha floor fill so fast and hell yeah my ass was front and center! "Do dat shit gurl!" Some chick yelled in my ear. I started to blast on her, until I noticed it was tha broad from earlier. With a nod we both started freakin' it. Next thing I know, an argument starts between her and two big bitches with fucked up weaves. You know, when you wear the shit so long it's not only dry as fuck and nappy, but tha glue's so old it don't hold tha track so tha shits lifted and hangin' by a strand; and the other has Cornflakes, Skittles candy, Juicy Fruit wrappers and multiple colors in it. Hysterical! I must've blanked, cause they started scrappin', to be little. she was handlin' bigums so her twin decided to jump in. I couldn't let that go down so I grabbed Cornflakes, added a bowl, spoon and the milk too! And from that day on, Dove and I hung out. I knew she was sneaky, conniving and would fuck a cow if it gave her the eye. But to blatantly have Kione show up, dats right I said Kione, not my son, dat lil ninja deserved whateva I decided would be his punishment for purposely havin' sex with me. Dove's ass was dirty for not comin' to me with the info from jump. That showed and told me Dove's ass ain't a friend or associate, her ass was jealous and a straight hater. Best believe both my eyes will be watchin', my ears tuned to every word Dove says and doesn't say. * Dove tossed the garbage bags inside an over flowin' dumpster, then jumped back; heart racin' when the bag fell and some filthy homeless guy climbed out with a bag fulla cans. "Jeezus Crackers! You scared the shit outta me! Fuck you doin?!" Dude was hideous! Matted, filthy hair, dirty ass face, a mouthful of brown, furry teeth and clothin' that looked like he'd worn a year straight, all surrounded by funk so strong her eyes watered and nose burned. Fuck, tha garbage smelled better than his ass! "You got some bottles and cans in dat bag?" he asked. Dove's legs wobbled from the stench oozing from everywhere. "Hell, yo ass already stink, you already in the garbage; look fo' yo damn self." Turnin' she speed walked back to her apartment. runnin' smack into Aisha and her daughter. 'Here we go.' thought Dove' accessin' Aisha who wore Escada jeans and blue Escada short sleeved shirt, Gucci sandals on her feet; while her lil monkey sported a For All Mankind romper and YSL kiddie cage sandals on pedicured feet. 'Bernard never dressed me or Jeff half as nice. Fuckin' loser.' Aisha smirked as if hearin' Dove's thoughts. "Hi Ms. Mitchell." greeted Jeffica all nice and sweet. 'Gag me.' thought Dove then forced out a "Sup." past tight lips. "Honey didn't mommy tell you not to speak to tha triflin'. Once you do, they'll get all in yo business or want somethin'." "Sorry mommy." she mumbled, while Dove steamed and debated on takin' it to her heavily made up face. Aisha sniffed, sniffed again, held her nose, then she and her rat backed up a step. "Fuck is that smell? Honey you've sunk to a whole new low, a smelly one." Dove reached out and touched her with a solid blow to tha eye. Jeffica screamed, then started cryin' like she'd just saw her ugly ass momma gunned down or some shit. "You broke ass, dusty, stinkin' bitch!" Aisha swung back, catchin' Dove with a two piece to lip and chin. Now Dove was the one stumblin' and tripped over a rock; fell on her ass and had no choice but to ball up when a flurry of kicks came her way. "Hoe! If you ever feel froggy and put hands on me when I got my daughter, I'll fuckin' murder you out here!" bellowed Aisha, damn near foamin' at the mouth she was so angry. "Come on baby." cooed Aisha, took her hand and walked off without a backwards glance. * Furious, Dove stared at bruised chin and swollen cut bottom lip. "Fuckin' hatin' hoe tried to tear up my face cause she's an ugly, wart hog lookin' bitch." muttered Dove just as a knock sounded at the door. Stompin' to the door, Dove bypassed the peephole, only to wish she had when Bernard caught her with a left. Dove flew backwards, slid across the floor and thunked her head on the coffee table leg. Seeing stars, moons and clovers, Dove blinked a few times to bring shit back into focus. By the time her vision fully cleared, a fist was flying towards her face. Cheek exploding with pain, Dove screamed, kicked her feet, wind milled her arms, doing anything to keep Bernard's pyscho ass off her. Blows rained down as Bernard yelled. Dove, losing consciousness heard words that sounded like he spoke under water. * When she awoke, Dove was dizzy as hell, as if she'd drank a liter of booze to the face, with no chaser. Wincing, Dove made to sit up, only to cry out in pain when her ribs protested. "Fuck happened?" Noticing it was dark outside from open blinds, Dove slowly stood on wobbly legs. Face and body throbbin', she slowly made her way down the hall and into her bathroom. Flickin' on the light, Dove stared at herself in disbelief, then burst into tears. Cryin' hurt, but the devastation that was her face, she couldn't help but to cry. Swollen cheeks, puffy lips, top and bottom split down the middle, dried blood crusted both nostrils, one eye was swellin' and turnin' colors, the other, a fiery red. A deep scratch, like from a ring, graced the middle of her forehead. Leanin' closer to the mirror, Dove cringed in horror, the letter B from Bernard's ring. Fresh tears fell, makin' her eyes sting and burn. Turnin' on the shower, Dove slowly stripped, then gasped anew at the Timberland insignia imprinted on her stomach. Payback begin to simmer as Dove stepped beneath warm water. Bernard had no right getting' involved in-between she and Aisha's beef; to come to her home and beat on her like she was a man. "Bitch! You hit my daughter!" Dove jumped, almost slippin' and fallin' on the tubs slick surface as Bernard's words he'd shouted earlier came back loud and clear, along with others. "I never loved you. I used you for a place to stay until Aisha got her apartment." and "Jeff ain't my son hoe, you get around. Take out an ad, cause it fo' damn sure ain't me!" "You wanna play Bernard? Okay, let's play!" screamed Dove. Steppin' out, Dove dried off, pulled open her medicine cabinet, bypassin' Xanax, Paxil and Thioxanthenes to snatch a bottle of Morphine she'd gotten from Taylor. Twistin' open the cap revealed two pills. "Fuck! Fuck! Fuck!" Dove slammed the mirrored cabinet open and closed so hard the mirror shattered. Why was everyone against her? She was tryin' to be nice, but mafuckas were pushin' all her buttons. Starin' blindly at the shards in the sink, Dove picked up a piece, then jabbed it into her forearm twice. Blood ran down her arm and dripped into the sink. A small smile formed. *

CHAPTER 6

Joshua lived out in Bristol, up a huge, twisty hill. His home was surrounded by fruit trees which gave off a delicious scent as we pulled up his driveway. "Your home is lovely, it looks so peaceful." Josh chuckled. "It's too peaceful. Hopefully I can get you out here more often, until you agree to stay." Whoa Nelly! Reign dat shit in potna, cause Taylor lives with me, myself and I okay. You'll never get the chance to put my black ass out. I'm just sayin'. Joshua pushed a button, his garage door rose, showin' a motorcycle, and a cute ass dark pink Buick Enclave Suv. Her sexy ass had my kitty moister den a mug. Whoa..wait one big panties on the clothesline minute. Didn't he just tell me he lived alone and had asked me to stay not even five seconds a damn go? So whose car was this? See, dats why I'm all 'bout self; I gets mines and get gone unless its sumthin' in it for me to go anotha round. I'm like be honest wit cho shit boo, no need to lie. Shit, we can still do the nasty, feel me. Shit, if more chicks were on my level, instead of catchin' feelins' and wantin' to beat up every chick dat looks at cho man, which makes no sense by the way; cause soon as yo backs turned, he'll be fuckin' in tha corner, talkin' 'bout 'she felt weak bae. I was helpin' her up'. Please, chile get cho life back boo. That's all I'm sayin'. Josh parked and didn't say shit 'bout tha car, so neither did I. Hopefully dinner wouldn't take long 'cause Jarvis was pickin' me up at midnight. Say what chu feel, but you can never say Taylor's broke, beggin, and borrowin; okay. Enterin' his home through the kitchen I was impressed by all the bells and whistles. Josh showed me around his four bedroom, three and a half bath, basement converted into an office, home. He led me into a small nook, where an oval table sat dressed for two. Aww how sweet, now ninja let's eat. Momma got balls to gargle and dick to suck, I'm just sayin'. * "D..damn girl, w..where you been?" stammered Omaire. Stayin' away from yo stutterin' ass. I ain't tryina overdose on y.y..you and start s..s..stutterin' too. Let me stop. Smirk. 'Ccause tha dicks good and the money's even better, so I played nice. "Aww, did you miss this good lovin?" I teased, lickin' pouty lips, flavored with cherry lip Glass; then slid hands down full plump breasts, gave 'em a squeeze, slid down taut belly and patted juicy cat. Omaire nodded, thank God, sparin' my ears the job of weedin' out all the extra letters to get to the meat of what he's tryina say. "Well I'm here now boo." I cooed, reached out and lightly gripped hard dick tentin' his slacks and moaned. Not even remotely horny, I faked that shit. I actually had cramps, so playin' around and fuckin' were the furthest things on my mind, but when money calls, yo girl always answers. Believe that. Hey, maybe I should run a few classes on dis shit, not for free cause ain't jack free, not even a courtesy cup of water at McDonald's, I'm just sayin'. "Stop p..playin' Tay', s..s..suck my d..dick." "You got it daddy." Kneelin' right there in the foyer, I unzipped chocolate slacks, pushed 'em to his ankles along with boxers and gasped. Dis ninja had tied a yellow ribbon round the head of his dick, loopin' a blingin' ass ring threw the bow, which rested on top. I done seen it all, was the shit cuttin' off circulation? And what'd he do, jerk his meat til it got hard enough, then tied it? Had he walked around for hours like dat? And what if I had been a no show? Would he have slept wit it? And how'd he pee, cause I don't want no ring dat smells like urine on my fuckin' finger. You know how hard it'd be to clean all the grooves and shit. Rollin' my eyes I oohed and aahed, all while thinkin' Ty's ring costed more. "I love it." I gushed, almost gaggin' on that one; untied the ribbon, opened wide and got busy. Look ma, no hands! Smirk. Peekin' at my wrist watch, it was twelve thirty. Now watch boys and girls, pay close attention: jaws cavin' in and out I sucked, deep throatin', swirlin' my tongue all around the head, underside, then teased the slit, slob coated shaft from base to tip, lips smackin'. I sucked, slobbed and bobbed until Johnson swole, pulsed and warm salty snot like cum shot out. I let a lil dribble down my lips, blew a cum bubble, swallowed and looked at the time; twelve thirty-seven. I'm a monster at this. I burped, stood, looked at Omaire's tremblin' legs and thought, 'You need more fruits and veggies nigga, cause yo sperm taste like a bunch of oysters left in tha sun too long. I'm just sayin'. * I stopped at the corner store for my usual sweets run and since Manny's was closed, I triple checked traffic then crossed the street and went inside the twenty-four hours corner store. That shit was packed, like everybody and they momma were inside, havin' sandwiches made, buyin' beer, snacks and loosies. "Well damn, it ain't tha weekend, nor is it check day." I grumbled, then sauntered ova to the snacks and grabbed Smartfood, that's some good ass popcorn. A bag of Lay's chips, a small pack of Chips Ahoy then over to the counter where I got a box of jawbreakers, peppermint balls, two Paydays and a M&M plain. Don't judge what I eat, cause munchin' on monkey nuts and chicken feet stew is gross as hell. Anyhoo, who comes strollin' in? Donell's ole loud, flamboyant ass. Now Taylor loves the gays okay, they're some cool mafuckas to be friends with, just don't be all extra and try to do me boo; 'cause I serve tha gays to huntie. I'm just sayin'. Donell smelled like he'd bathed in Fatale, I own a bottle and trust, a little goes a long way. Some chunky ass Manolos on feet that looked soft as cotton and smooth as silk, up calves that were hella muscled, like he leg lifted weights. A lime green skirt with a slit that allowed glimpses of a hairy thigh, up to a belly that looked four months pregnant and a halter top, stop..pause. Shave yo chest boo. How you walkin' round wit' 34C boobs and enough hair to make a wig on yo chest? Dat shit ain't cute okay. Do one or the other, cover it or shave. Jeezus crackers wit cheese, who in tha hell wants a mouthful of titty chest hair? His arms were tatted up, his nails nicely done with gel nails; each wrist held bracelets, up to his face which was beat to tha gawds. Shit, I need to hit up whoever does Donell's make-up. Five piercings in one ear, two in the other; one of those bars through his nose, a stud under his bottom lip which were in full out, as Donell stepped fully inside flippin' Remy hair off his shoulder. Violet colored contacts latched onto me, followed by a beamin' smile that revealed pearly whites and twin dimples. "Hey Tay, what's up girlie? Don't chu know no good?" Hunh? "Uh, hey girl, how you doin'?" I said in return. "Nothin' much, on my way to a Trade Party girl. Gotta get that money, first of the month's 'round the corner." "I know that's right." Donell strutted over to the fridge, slid it open and grabbed a Red Bull and a can of Coke. "You settle down yet Tay'? I know you got mofos comin' at chu left n right." my face twisted as I moved up in line. "Girl we cool, so I'ma say this as nice as possible; don't curse me boo.

I ain't lookin' to be tied down..at all..ever. Men are only good for an hour or three before they expire like milk; and we both know it stinks. It's clumpy and when you dump it, tha smell lingers no matter how much you scrub the sink or spray Lysol." Donell burst out laughing. "I know that's right." Another few steps in line. "So Donell, where's yo boo thang? He must not have a problem wit' you goin' to Trade Parties?" "My boo? What boo hunny? Please, I slay 'em wit' da ill na na, collect dem coins and I'm out. I don't do boo's, niggas play too damn much. All dat I luv you bae, we'll go public eventually or you mean the world to me.... girl please. I'd end up slicin' and dicin', alright!" She dragged out the latter. "So you and Jermaine aren't togetha'?" Donell arched a brow, smacked her lips and said, "Hell no! Ah uhn girl, dat boys confused on who he is. One minute he's blowin' up my cell wit' all dat bae I miss you crap, tha next its, "I like pussy"; fuck outta here. Then you at my door pleadin' n shit; "Bae I miss you, I'm sorry". Then he wildin'. Girl I'm straight on Mr. Jermaine's confused ass." Snapped Donell. Laughin', I stepped up and put my stuff on the counter, when the bell over the door chimed. Who should walk in, the topic of our conversation; Jermaine's ass. "Here we go." muttered Donell with a hard eye roll and tooth suck. Jermaine walked right up on Donell and punched her in the face. The fuck!? Donell fell back and would've knocked me down if I hadn't scrambled out the way. "Oh no you didn't mothafucka! Don't nobody lay hands on me, unless dey payin'! I ain't yo punchin' bag bitch!" shrieked Donell, who flung her items and started throwin' blows. Donell might act girly, but her ass fought like a straight nigga; taggin' Jermaine's ass wit' crazy combos that knocked his ass into the chip rack. They both fell, Jermaine hopped up, scooped Donell and tossed her ass into the freezer that held ice cream. "Aww sukey." sang Shelly as she came through the door, eyes wide. Dude behind the counter was yellin' n shit to no avail as they tore Twenty-four up! I pulled out my cell, hit record and taped the happenins'. Some big headed bastard came inside, snatched up Jermaine in a full nelson givin' Donell free reign to fuck Donell up if she so chose. Spittin' a wad of blood on the floor, Donell whipped out a straight razor so fast, I ain't know where tha shit came from. Donell walked up so close, breasts met chest. The two glared at each other. "I should gut cho ass and twerk on yo intestines nigga. Last warnin', stay tha fuck away from me Jermaine. I give two snakes pussy on givin' you anotha chanc. Move on Jermaine, before tha only place you're moved to is the morgue." Folding the razor, Donell walked out the door, dude holdin' Jermaine smacked him atop his head with a can of Spam, knockin' his ass out cold before makin' an exit. *

CHAPTER 7

"Took yo behind so long to answer tha door?" Griped Dove. "You in there fuckin'?" Glenda giggled. "Nah, I was tellin' lil Marvin I love him. He just left, so I was probably outside when you knocked." Dove took a seat on the couch. "Are you and his sexy ass daddy gettin' along better?" Glenda snorted. "Could be better if his wife didn't erk my nerves." Dove laughed. "Girl, play tha game. Overdose her with nothin' but kindness, that'll freak her ass out." Glenda laughed. "Anyway, what's been up wit' you? Catch me up to speed." Dove sighed all dramatically. "What hasn't happened girl? Sometimes I wonder why I even try. You know, like why bother." Glenda had never heard Dove sound so morose before. Not sure what to say, she just nodded instead. "Well I'm sure you already know that Bernard and Aisha are back together. He found out Jeff wasn't his and threatened to hurt me and him if he saw us anywhere near his precious mother." Glenda gaped in disbelief. She knew how Dove only told half the story, always choosin' to leave out what she'd done to get to the point where someone had turned on her. "I know, right. Then I see Aisha and their rat of a daughter...." "Wait. I thought Bernard said that lil girl wasn't his?" Dove clapped her hands. "Exactly! Now all a sudden she's his seed. Anyway, me and dat bitch exchange words, so I pop off and hit her ass; her daughter jumps in.." Glenda gasped, "I know, she's a kid. You know I love kids, I'd never purposely hurt a kid. So somehow I trip over the lil r....girl and fall. Aisha starts kickin' and stompin' me while her kid is bitin' me.." "No!" "Yes girl, then she yells she's gonna tell B and storms off." Glenda jumped up, raced into the kitchen and returned with a bottle of Bacardi dark and a no name bottle of soda, then poured two glasses. "So I go home to access tha damage, there's a knock at the door. I swung it open to a vicious punch in tha face. It's Bernard and he's pissed like I've never seen before." Tears streamed down Dove's face. Truthfully, when she picked up her glass, she quickly poked herself in both eyes with a fingernail coated in hot sauce. "Punches, kicks, stomps, he even stabbed me in the arm." "I know you still care for Bernard, but I truly hope you went to the hospital so they could've documented your injuries. His ass needs to be behind bars." snapped Glenda. Dove sniffed and wiped her eyes. "I did. It was the hardest thing

I've ever done." lied Dove. Glenda patted her leg. "Well stay strong Dove, you've done nothin' wrong. You're the victim here, so screw how anyone else feels." A wavery smile. "Thanks Glenda, you're a true friend. I'm glad to have you in my life." "No need to thank me." she hesitated. "Does Taylor know?" Dove shrugged. "I doubt it, I haven't been outside until today. I didn't answer any calls or knocks." Again Glenda stayed silent. "Well, I'm gonna call her, see if she's home." Dove finished her drink and poured herself another. "Hllo." I sang, dancin' behind the mop to the sounds of IHeart Memphis' 'Lean and Dab' playin' on the radio. "Hey Tay, it's Glenda. You busy?" I started to tell Glenda hell yeah, but I'd just finished cleanin' so why not go hang out. "Nope, what's good?" "Well Dove's here, can you come over?" Oh Lord, I hope this ain't another so called intervention, cause her name ain't Sally Jesse and I ain't in tha audience hung up on her every word. "Sure, on my way." Hangin' up, I poured out mop water, rinsed the mop and walked into the livin' room. Grabbing keys and twenty bucks off top of the TV, I turned off the radio, and bounced. Soon as I stepped outside, heat attacked me in shimmery waves. The usual goin's on were goin on as I trooped it past Rosalie's, my nose wrinklin' at the smell of some part of tha pig bein' cooked. Now, I love pork, ham, bacon, chittlins', but you gotta know whatcha doin' cuse errbody can't cook or clean 'em. Example, one Thanksgivin'

I stopped over 'she who shall not be named' and was offered a plate. What black person you know gonna turn down free food? 'Nough said. So anyhoo she sets a plate fulla food before me, smellin' all yummy n shit. Greens, homemade mac n cheese, macaroni salad, rice, homemade stuffin', chittlin;, you name it, it was on my plate. So I scoop up some greens and start chewin'; and I'm crunchin' and chewin' like da fuck is up wit' dese greens? Ole girl hadn't let 'em cook long enough so they were tough and chewy. Then I reach in my mouth to grab what I figure is a piece a bone, dirt, fuckin' dirt! How you don't wash 'em before throwin' 'em in da pot?! Okay, so onto tha mac n cheese. It had no flavor whatsoever. It looked like she'd used cottage cheese instead of blocked cheese, so I'm like strike two. I pick up a chittlin' and its huge, like she didn't bother to cut 'em. I take a nibble and its salty as fuck, so I fling it back on the plate and I see all this nasty shit on it. I go in a lil closer...dis non cookin' hoe hadn't cleaned 'em; aww hell naw! I'm done, finished. She sets down a nice sized turkey, I ain't fuckin' wit' it cause obviously she needs MAJOR help in tha damn kitchen. When I look between the turkey's legs lookin' for stuffin' and see the giblet bag, I'm done! So Rosalie cookin' tha pig actually had me kinda grossed out as I passed. Openin' Glenda's screen, I stepped inside to the sounds of Glenda consolin' Dove. Eye roll. Drum roll please. I guarantee this girl done somethin' and twisted it around to make herself the damn victim. Nobody gives a hoot sweetie okay. You do shit, it rolled down hill and slapped you in the face. I get a glimpse of bruises even Maybeline can't hide and think, damn! You got beat tha fuck up! Beat down to the seams. Ump, lips so big she can kiss her own ass, ha! I'm just sayin'. "Girl what shit storm did you encounter?" Dove cried a lil harder. "Tay! That wasn't very nice." she admonished. This from a chick Dove lied on and had beat up and hospitalized. "Yeah, yeah. I never said I was nice. Now what happened?" I asked again while noticin' this trick peekin' between her fingers. Hmm, well whoever tagged that ass did a number on her. She had bruises up and down both arms and what looked like a cut on her forearm. Glenda lifted her shirt and pointed at another which kinda looked like a fadin' boot print, and I can't forget them raccoon eyes she sported. "Aisha and Bernard did this." said Glenda, then quickly ran down the events leadin' up to her lookin' like the bride of Chucky. "So what you gone do Dove? I know you ain't gone take that beat down and let shit rock." Before she could tune up them lyin' ass lips her cell rang, Glenda scooped it off the table, eyes wide when she saw who was callin'. "It's Bernard." Glenda lowly stated, like he could hear her. Dove stiffened. "Put it on speaker phone." Doing as told, Glenda set the phone back on the table. "You're dead Dove, you hear me! Yo ass done fucked wit the wrong one. you called DCF on me and my gurl?! They took my kid and arrested Aisha when she bust the worker in the head wit' her high heeled shoe." Dove burst out laughin'. "Yeah, ha ha. Now, be dead later." click. We all stared silently at each other. * We all decided to go chill at Keney Park. Normally I don't step a cute foot up in that mafucka, cause every time you turn around someone's fightin' and gets stabbed. Someone's shootin' and ends up dead, or you're stumblin' across a dead body, up in the trees (how they do that shit), dead on the slide, dead in the pool; everywhere you turn. The shit was serious. But since I still hadn't seen nor heard from Aaron, I'd see if he was up there watchin' his brethren playin' soccer. Dove parked all crazy. Thankfully no one was next to her take two parkin' spots ass. Jumpin' out, I dug boy short undies out my crack and followed Glenda and Dove across lush green grass. The park was poppin'. The scent of grilled meats scented the air, children laughed and played, then made dashes towards the arrivin' Good Humor truck while some young adults played ball or speed walked towards the pool open all summer long. Others leaned against cars, shootin' the shit while whistlin' every half minute at passin' curvy flesh on display. "So far so good," I think aloud, but trust and believe, it only took one mafucka to set shit off. The soccer game was in progress when we strolled up and took seats on hard ass bleachers. Squintin' through the sun's rays blindin' a bitch, I looked around tryina spot Aaron's ass when his boy Antwon aka Won saw me and walked over. Won is a sexy mafucka. Tall, blemish free skin, a nice facial edge up and a head fulla waves. He dressed nice, smelled nice; he even had no problem givin' a chick tha dough. Won's issue, his breath was kickin'. Beath so bad, I look forward to a far. Breath so stink, he's literally talkin' shit. I'm just sayin'. Anyhoo, Won had been offerin' to sponsor a sista, but no way could I fuck that cause the first inhale, my whole body would just dry up leavin' nothin' but ashes. "Aww shit, here comes yuk mouth." whispered Dove all loud and shit. I know stanky pus' ain't tryin' it. "Hey Taylor, how you doin'?" he greeted. Shit, I was fine til yo ass walked ova. Now I'm sittin' here holdin' my breath. "Good, how you been?" was my answer. "Hey Dove." she nodded and whispered somethin' to Glenda. They both stood and headed towards a snack truck with its menu written into its paint. "We'll be right back Tay'." Glenda said, gave Won another look and started across the field. "Is Aaron here?" A surprised look slid across his face. "Why you lookin' at me like that Won?" He exhaled and I swear my forehead and eyebrows caught fire. "Aaron got deported back to St. Lucia." "What? Since when? Why? What happened?" slid rapidly out. "He got caught transportin' two hundred kilos. The government locked him up at first, out in New York since that's where he was when he got busted. Then changed their minds and had ICE come scoop him. He had his wife call me to let me know he made it home. From my understandin' he's bein' detained until the U.S. and St. Lucia can come to an agreement." Well damn! I ain't know Aaron was doin' it big like that! "Wow! No I didn't know, I thought he was just busy or had lost his phone or sumthin'." "Anyway, now that Aaron's out tha picture, what's up with me and you? I know you like the finer things and money's probably tight right now." Oh no he didn't insinuate I'm a broke bitch and on the prowl for my next vic. First of all, I'm always on the prowl for that, cause you can never have enough dick and dollas in yo life. Second, even if I was, I wouldn't touch Won's ass. Getcho hygiene up boo before you step to a bitch of my caliber, okay doo doo breath. Mouth smell like you carryin' a corpse around; fuck outta here. "Nah, I'm straight Won, thanks though." I could see Dove and Glenda finally on their way back across the grass. Thank the breath mint Gods cause I'm reat to go fo' real. When dis ninja said, "Oh you one of those stuck up bitches that think she's too good for a nigga. Bitches like you make a man beat you til you act right." My jaw dropped in astonishment, the switch jiggled. "Word, dats how you feelin' hunh?" I stood up and eyed Won. "Nigga please, yo ass put hands on me, it'll be the last thing you EVER do in this life, and dats probably what yo ass has to do in order to get a chick to fucks wit' yo tart breath ass. Now step tha fuck off ya bumba rasclad sien!" Won's yellow skin turned a bright red. See, yellow ninjas always think the sun rises and sets on they ass, not! That's why I prefer dark meat or some caramel sweetness on my tongue. I'll do yellow if the cash is right, but dis jealous, woman beatin' bastard got me all tha way fucked up. Mad I'd left my purse wit' brass knuckles in Dove's car, I backed up a step, cause I knew dis shits 'bout to be on like hot buttered popcorn. Glenda and Dove walked up; Dove eatin' chicken, Glenda a hotdog, a small cardboard tray in hand, holdin' another order of wings and onion rings wrapped half assed in tin foil. "We got you some.." Dove trailed off. Seein' irate look on my face she sighed, sat her food on the bleachers and spat, "Sup, is there a problem over here?" Glenda, busy eatin', finally looked up mid chew, eyes wide and froze. "Mind ya fuckin' manners you slut. Matter fact, go finish suckin' off tha food man for that shit chu eatin'." Won growled, pure annoyance in his tone. People in the park heard and noticed the commotion and drew closer. "Listen shitty diaper mouth, you mad cause my girl turned you down, oh well stinky, I'm sure you've heard that on numerous times. Why don't you stop at the dentist on yo way home. You're gonna need a miracle, but hopefully he can do somethin', cause dat halitosis is horrible!" boomed Dove. "Fuck you!" Won gave an emotional yell, soundin' like tears clogged his throat, then swung, catchin' Glenda who hit the ground snorin'. Tha fuck!

Glenda hadn't said a word to Won's triflin' ass, but you swing on her? Where they do that at? Before Dove and I could double team his ass, some dude came outta nowhere flyin' through the air with an elbow to the top of Won's head. Won folded like he had noodle legs, only to get stomped once he hit the grass. Blood dribbled down his forehead, then shot out his mouth when dude stomped him in the sternum. Ump, whoeva dude was, as I stood behind him, was cut up better than a bag of the best dope. Shirt off, I drooled at the cobra back, tapered waist and a huge scorpion stretchin' across it. Barely breathin' hard, dude turned and I felt my heart seize. Hex... *

CHAPTER 8

"Girl yo ass been tight lipped since we left Won's ass laid out at the park." said Dove as the three of us chilled at Glenda's. Her nose wasn't broken, but it was swollen and definitely sore. "Give up tha juice girl, spill all the tea. Who was that sexy damsel in distress rescuer, cause I gots to get to know him." Chattered Dove which was seriously gettin' on my last damn nerve okay. I'm like damn bitch, if I wanted to tell yo ass 'bout Hex, I would've done it all damn ready. Talkin' my fuckin' ears off won't get me to tellin', it will get cho ass cursed da hell out and put tha fuck out. Glenda appeared wit' a wad of tissue in hand, and a twisted piece stuffed up both nostrils. "I can't tell if under my eyes are changin' colors." she said soundin' nasally as fuck. Dove stared, then frowned. "Fuck all dat, ask Tay' to give up the info on Mr. Sexy. Don't you want to thank him fo' savin' yo life?" "Dove relax, dude ain't the best thing since dildos. Yo ass 'bout to cum on yoself if you haven't already. You that damn desperate?" I asked. "Hell no I ain't cum, well maybe a lil. I'm tryina put tha rest all over that dick he's packin', but chu bein' real shady right now. What's he, an ex? Wait....that ain't dude from the Fed Pen is it?" She rattled on, makin' my head pound and temples throb. "Your eyes are fine Glenda, just take one of those percs I gave you. Don't be greedy though, cause I'm out til I luck up on another connect." I said, iggin' Dove's ass. Dove opened her mouth, then snapped it shut. Thank God, cause tha switch was 'bout to flip on motor mouth, fo' real. Standin', I made my way to the door. "I'm 'bout to go make somethin' to eat. I'll stop by tomorrow." and with that I left, unaware that eyes watched my exit. * Bubbles. Check. Body wash. Check. Checkin' the water's temperature with my big toe, I stepped in, sat down and sighed as the day's tension floated away. Too bad I couldn't get Hex out my thoughts as easily. I grudgingly admitted that Hex was cuter then he'd been back in the day. Back then everythin' 'bout him rubbed me the wrong way; his over eagerness to please, his voice, the way I'd catch him studyin' me, as if preparin' for a history exam, but once he sang like the stool pigeon he is, that rubbin' turned to hate. Just hearin' his name raised my blood pressure significantly. And here he was, appearin' out of thin air to defend me against a woman beater. It sounded like fodder for a Harlequin romance book. Knocks at the door broke into my thoughts scarin' the shit outta me. Water and bubbles splashed on the blue and cream rug sittin' before the tub. Standin' with a curse, I grabbed a fluffy towel, wrapped it around my sudsy wet frame. Stepped out and picked up my bathrobe, slipped it on and made my way to the door. "I'm fuckin' comin'! Quit bangin' like you the damn po-po!" If it's Rosalie's ole good beggin' ass bangin' like that, I'ma chop her in the damn wind pipe. I'm just sayin'. "Who tha hell is it?!" I shouted. Hearin' nothin', I gave a look through the peephole and saw flowers, with the sun settin' behind them. It really was a postcard moment. Too bad I don't do flowers or plants boo. So if you're tryina impress me you gotta come harder; perfume, an outfit, a nice ass pair of heels. Openin' the door, I felt my pressure rise once again when the flowers, white roses, lowered revealin' Hex on my doorstep. Face twisted, I blocked entrance and glared. "Fuck you want? And how you know I live here?!" I snapped. "Well hello to you too Taylor. Can I come in?" "Hell to tha no. Whatchu want nigga? Say whatchu need to, then turn around and bounce; and take dem wack ass rose's witchu." Hex smiled, "Still the same mean ass Taylor I see." deep sigh, I made to close the door, only for it to be halted by Hex's foot. "Five minutes, just five minutes and

I'll leave. Please Taylor." "Fine, once you step foot across the threshold the clock starts tickin'." "Deal." agreed Hex; smile disclosin' a small gap between front teeth. Closin' then lockin' the door, I made sure my robe was tightly secured, turned and ended up in a serious lip lock. Hmm, what to do..should I bite his fuckin' lips off? Should I kiss him back? Nah. So I stood there, stiff as hell, tongue not participatin' until he drew back wit' a groan, I'm like well damn boo, yo ass groanin' now; imagine if I gave a lil tongue action. Hex would probably swallow his tongue and if I put dis nana on him, he'd lose his mind! "Are you done? Four minutes and countin'." Hex raised a brow. Guess his kisses always get a different response. Oh well, kiss now, cry lata. "Damn, still icy hearted I see; it's cool. I'm back in town for a few, openin' a coupla spots and I need a promotor, interested?" "And what exactly would I be required to do? And how much you payin'?" Hex smiled, then took a seat and examined his nails. "Promote. You know, word of mouth. You know hella peeps. Anyway, at the club you'd cater only to VIP; get 'em spendin' every night, pick an expensive drink, work yo magic. If you can, invite a bunch of people, flyers, radio Facebook, Instagram, whateva. The otha spots a strip club, you'd do the same shit. Look sexy, smell good, get them niggas hype on seein' tha girls." he shrugged, "Whateva it takes." "Two and a half." "I'll pay two g's a night; if it's a full house three or more." My ears perked up. Okay, now you're speakin' my language. "Sounds good, but I need everythin' in writin'" Hex smirked. "Hw's Mason?" Ohh, I see what this is..dudes tryina scope out if Mason and I kept in touch. He was fishin' to see if I knew he was a dirty, squealin' rat. I smiled, walked up on Hex, then stood between his legs; untied my robe and let the towel drop. Perky breasts stood at attention, nipples on hard stared like twin laser beams, entrancing Hex like whoa. He licked his lips. "Damn ma yo body is perfect." Yawn, I know nucca, and if I didn't yo lustin' ass is proof enough. Hex slowly reached out and lightly ran a finger from hip to neck. "Yo skin so soft." he said, wonder all in his voice. Jeez, whatchu lay down wit' alligator skinned bitches? "Mmm, you like dat daddy?" I purred, turned and made 'em clap. "Hell yeah. I always wondered you know, but Mason's my boy.." "And yo ass will keep wonderin', this is as close as you'll ever get; and if I decide to work with you, that's all it'll ever be. So suck yo tongue back in, blink before yo eyes dry out and your outta minutes." I happily told his ass. Hex stared for a hot second, stood and strode toward the door. "The club opens next Friday, I'll have someone bring you the contract." *

"Have you thought about my proposal?" Asked Ty. We laid in bed, all snugly after a sweaty, whose gonna tap out first round of sex and he ruined it with this bullshit. Deep sigh. Why can't I just get some dick and let that be all it is? Why it's gotta be feelin's involved and shit. I'm just sayin'. "No not really, I've been kinda busy." Ty rolled his eyes. "Busy doin' what? Fuckin' otha dudes? I'm offerin' stability Tay. I thought every girl/woman wanted the white dress." I thought with a voice box Ty wouldn't say much, sheeit, dis mofo was holdin' dat box to his neck and speakin' so fast his words were runnin' together; so I'm hearin', 'mofferinstability' which was hilarious! Bitin' my cheek to keep from laughin', I tried to think of anythin' not to laugh, but the shit slipped out anyway. You ever laugh so hard you cry and fart, well babyy, it was one of dem long ass farts too. Poot...pop..pop.. annnt! Ty looked at me all kinds of crazy, like he couldn't believe I just cut loose durin' a serious conversation. Well believe it nucca, cause if yo ass wasn't standin' here tryina scream on a bitch through a voice box, tha fart would've never happened. I'm just sayin'. "Sorry. Look Ty, honestly I'm not lookin' for commitment. I'm not tha chick who dreams of ownin' a home, havin' a dog and three point one kids, whateva tha hell that means. I like things tha way they are now. We kick it, have sex, kick it and I take my ass on." Hard eyes grilled me before Ty finally gave a head nod. "Okay. That's cool, if that's how you want it." "It is." I slid from bed and started gettin' dressed, 'cause

I could hear the 'its best we end things' speech comin'. Yeah I'd miss tha dick, and his pussy eatin' skills even more, but most of all I'll miss tha cash and gifts Ty loves to toss my way. Oh well, there's always more dicks in the sea. * Check day rolled around and everyone was out and about, eagerly awaitin' the arrival of that blue, white and red truck. School was officially over, so kids were outside causin' all kinds of mayhem. Mabel, dis old, crabby bitch who lived towards the back of Nelton Court, had just hung wet sheets on the line; when Mario on his new dirt bike revved the engine, kickin' up dirt all over her sheets before poppin' a wheelie laughin' hysterically and pullin' off. Cream, dis hot ass sixteen year-old let two boys pull a train on her, then cried rape when neither gave her money for the new LeBron's. Just straight messy. Shelly came outside wheelin' Josephine, who looked ready to croak any minute. Rosalie waved in my direction, I gave her ass a nod and continued walkin' in no mood for bullshit today. I had cramps bad as hell and was on my way to Manny's for a box of Pamprin, or Midol if I couldn't sweet talk Louis outta couple of percs, which he sold behind his father's back. A bell signaled my arrival, surprise widened my eyes, the usual loud Spanish music had been replaced with R&B. Haltin', I gave a quick look around. I was definitely inside Manny's, only Manny wasn't behind the counter, some heavily made up

Spanish chick with blonde streaks, long curvin' nails and rings on every finger watched me watch her. "Whateva youngin." I uttered, turned and switched down the aisle, givin' her somethin' to watch, okay. Not findin' what I sought, I hit tha next aisle and ran smack into Louis who was stockin' shelves. "Sup papi." Louis looked around all nervous like, makin' my head swivel too. "Uh, hey Taylor. How you been?" Whoa Nelly, since when did we hold civil conversations? Usually his ass felt some type of way 'cause I played him around income tax time and didn't give up tha panty drawers. Pastin' on a smile, I sidled closer, licked my lips and whispered, "Better now that I've seen you. How you doin'?" All flustered, Louis gulped and nervously cleared his throat. The chick up front yelled somethin' in Spanish. Whateva she said had ole Louis back pedalin' like a mafucka. "I..I gotta go make a sandwich.." "Okay. So whose tha new chick and where's Manny?" "Oh....my father is home recuperating, he suffered a mild heart attack." I waited a beat, to hear who long nails was, but Louis' lips were sealed as he scurried down the aisle. Okayy. Grabbin' what I'd come for, I peeped some boy pocketin' shit out the corner of my eye. I'd never seen him before, which meant squat when people around here moved in and out on the daily. Headin' up front, I walked over to the lil section where sandwiches were made, opened my mouth to ask about doin' business when dis chick came from behind goin' off; they started arguin'. Louis hopped over tha counter and grabbed tha kid just as he opened tha door and escaped. "So.." My words were cut short when Louis spat, "I thought we were cool, but you send your brother to steal from my father while distracting me?!" Wait a hot damn minute, who did what now? The switch jiggled. "I don't know what da fuck ya'll bitchin' 'bout, but I ain't send nobody nowhere to steal nothin' boo; 'cause Taylor pays for hers." I held up a box of Pamprin and shook it. The chick started flowin' again, so I stepped to Cruella Deville and smiled. "English bitch. I know you speak it, you've got issue wit' me, so say whatchu feel. Don't hide behind a bunch of 'I no speakie de English' hoe." Big ass hazel eyes stretched to the limit. "I said I'm sick of you people coming in here askin' for credit. You never pay, steal from us and try and fuck our men." Ooo, she done took my black ass all the way there! "You racist fuckin' guala! I don't need to bring no one nowhere to distract a damn thang, why? Cause I'm never broke bitch! Ask 'bout me hoe fo' you assume anythin' 'bout me. As fo' dis ninja you got all jacked up, I don't know him or his mammy, but if I did, I'd let her ass know how you laid hands on her kid; and last bitch, I gets any dick I want, any race, anytime, anywhere. Don't be J cause yo mixed bag of body parts wants Louis and he only has eyes for me. Get cho life sweetie, practice on a dildo and when you build skills and confidence, try again. Until then back up off me!" Ole gurls face turned a range of colors while her mouth opened and closed with no words escapin'. Louis meanwhile had searched the kid, pulled out two Oreo cookies, two sunflower seeds and a Danish; tossed it atop the counter and pushed him out the door. "I'm sorry Taylor, you've never caused any problems in my father's store." "You damn right you sorry!" "Magda no!" shouted Louis, although a second too late. Ole gurl snuck my ass with a can of Beefaroni to the back. Ooo, I felt like the incredible hulk when I turned to serve ha ass, cramps be damned. "Ohh you wanna smack a bitch wit' Beefaroni hunh? Okay bitch, lets play." I said all calm; totally ignorin' Louis pleadin' not to fight, not to tear up his father's store. Not. When I'm done she'll have plenty of knots to ice, let's see, 'B' "Bitch!" Punch to her tit, and a twist of nipple. She shrieked and swung. I ducked and came up wit' one to her eye. 'E' "Every time I see you, be prepared to scrap." I told her, grabbed dem blonde streaks wound it round my fist and bought face to meet knee. 'E' "Eat dis ass whoopin'. How it taste? Dis whatchu get when you, 'F' fucks wit' da best. 'A' an uppercut, which snapped her head back. Louis knew better than to interfere, he'd seen me slice a nigga last summer for jumpin' in to help his girl. 'R' right cross to da jaw, blood spewed, slappin' Louis in tha face. She swung again and caught onto my ponytail, then tried to yank me to the ground. I widened my stance, lowered and flipped her over my shoulder. 'O' "only a non fightin' bitch wants to hair pull." I taunted, 'N' "Now stay down tramp fo' I really serve it to yo ass fo' disrespectin' me!" 'I' "If you see me again..." I dusted my hands, pulled out four singles and flung 'em in her fucked up face. "...yo ass betta turn around and hope I ain't spot yo beat down to tha ground, moanin' and cryin' fo' Louis to help you ass!" Snatchin' up my Pamprin I bounced. Oh yeah, I beat the BEEFARONI out Magda's ass!

CHAPTER 9

"I'm just sayin', why she's gotta be all tight lipped 'bout dude Glenda? Any other time Tay' could give a fuck 'bout a nigga, she cares less if one of us goes behind her back cause as she's put it numerous times;" Dove threw up quotations. "..she's secure wit' hers." Glenda slurped on her vanilla milkshake. "True, I just don't understand why you're so gung ho over this guy. What's goin' on with Jeff? Let's focus on that; if its meant for you and him to hook up, it will happen." Dove snorted, Glenda ever the pessimist was like a fingernail on a chalk board right now, irritatin' and makin' her flesh crawl. Dove gave an inpatient sigh. "Why you gotta be such a Debbie downer girl? Anyway, Brian and his fat cow of a girlfriend are refusin' to let me see Jeff. Do you know tha other day a fuckin' sheriff served me court papers? They're goin' after primary custody." Just sayin' it aloud pissed her off anew. "How dare Brian do that bum shit when he wasn't even a fuckin' father until I dropped him off over there." Glenda felt for her. She remembered how she'd felt when Marvin went behind her back and not only got full custody but he turned around and married his lawyer's assistant, supposedly. She frowned, rememberin' how hurt she'd felt. "Marvin fell for her while snatchin' my son away." "How can yo ass sit here and tell me to fight, when yo ass lost the battle too?" snapped Dove. Both stared at the other, lost in memories of heartaches and what ifs. * Toni and Kelly glared at each other, hatred gleamin' bright. It had been months and yet here they stood, both still bein' strung along by Brick; who claimed that he hadn't come to a decision yet on whom would officially become his main chick. Neither wanted to put voice to what they both feared, that Brick was usin' them; had pitted sister against sister for his own selfish reasons and had no intention on choosin' either one of them. Both missed the other, but would never admit it. "My dress looks nice on you." Toni said, tentativily throwing out an olive branch. "Thanks, you look nice too." responded Kelly. "So what do we do now?" they said as one, then laughed, took a few steps and hugged like only two sisters that forgive each other can. "We realize our potential and stop lettin' Brick play us. Besides,..." said Kelly, "the dicks good, but not good enough to make me hurt my sister; not anymore." They hugged again, the things they'd done to each other and said falling by the wayside. "Agreed." Toni giggled.

"There's a new strip joint openin' in four days; let's go audition, get this money and a new man." Kelly gave a thumbs up. "Let's do it." * Na-Nie On Deck, was Hex's new pride and joy. He'd come a long way since bein' Mason's yes boy, now he was the man. Bitches catered to his every whim no matter how outrageous; dudes would kiss his feet for a chance to be in his inner circle. After ratting on Mason and (NAME), the prosecuting attorney offered him a reduced sentence from twenty-five to life to seven years in a non-disclosed location where he'd do his time in protective custody. Some figured out who he was and tried him, only to end up in the prison infirmary. By the time Hex walked out a free man he'd shaved off his hair, grew a beard, picked up fifty pounds and converted it to hard muscle. On the streets he'd done a few lucrative jobs, invested here and there and voila! He owned three homes, a rack of cars, a restaurant, two clubs and now a strip club. Now all he needed was someone to share it with, and that someone was Taylor. Hex had a thing for Taylor, a serious thing. From the first time he'd laid eyes upon her he'd deemed Taylor his. So when an opportunity arose to get rid of Mason, he quickly did so. He waited til he had his shit together, tracked her down and made a play. Images of Taylor standing naked before him had fire racing straight between his legs. Soon. Soon Taylor would be his. * So, I'm goin' over this supposed contract of Hex's and my first thought was, why's it handwritten, kinda business you runnin? I'm just sayin'; when I hear a bunch of commotion outside. Rollin' my eyes I walked over to my kitchen window, peeped out and burst out laughin'. Reggae week was approachin' and damn near every rasta that lived in Nelton Court was outside, yellin', wavin' that colorful ass flag and dancin' to Spragga Benz and Foxy Brown's 'Tables Turn'. I'd totally forgotten about reggae week rollin' around. I definitely need to hit up tha mall for an outfit so I can drop it like it's hot, and scoop up another Jamaican to fill Aaron's empty spot. Ump, dem some hard strokin', booty lickin', pussy eatin', Mandingo slangin' bastards! Yess lawd, please provide me wit' some insides stretchin', dick in my ribs, can stroke nonstop for ninety minutes, tongue hangin' past his chin, strong back mafucka wit' deep pockets he ain't got no problem diggin' in. Amen. * Hexagon nite club and lounge. Hmm, I stared at Hex's club, three floors high and at least two blocks long; pulled open tha smoky grey door and stepped inside. People were walkin' everywhere, some shoutin' out orders to double check the lighting, the DJ was hookin' up speakers, then threw on Jon B for a test run; to the bartender who wiped down the bar and did a liquor count. He saw my approach licked his lips, slid a palm over his beard and smiled a welcome. "Hello there, I'm Adam. You here for the waitress position?" "Uh..no I'm the promotor. Came to take a quick look around, see what's what." Adam smiled, leaned on the bar and let black eyes run from head to toe. "Oh yeah? As good as you look you could promote anything and I'll buy." He flirted. Aww how sweet, he's flirtin'. Too bad I don't fuck bartender's, hol' up. I did give ole Brandon a taste didn't I? Well normally I don't. What can you do for me? Give me yo minimum wage check and a jar wit' a bunch of change he calls tips? Steal a coupla cases of booze? Nah boo, I'm good. "Cute. Is Hex around?" Adam wiggled his brows. "That lame can't please you like I can, believe that." Adam bragged. Really? Adam reminded me of a damn puppy; all eager, tail waggin', ignorin' all orders to sit and stay. Where's a rolled up newspaper when you need one...I'm just sayin'. "Taylor!" Adam jerked to attention, turned and resumed his liquor inspection. Issey Miyake assailed my senses as Hex walked up. Damn my pussy wet; and not cause a Hex, let's get that shit straight. I jus' love when a man smells good. "Hex, nice club from what I see." he smiled. "C'mon, let me show you around." There was a glass winding staircase which I headed for, until Hex led the way over to a big picture of some horse runnin' at the Kentucky Derby. Pushin' a button on a remote, the picture rose, revealin' a damn elevator! My jaw dropped 'cause I would've never guessed an elevator stood behind it. Wonderin' what other tricks Hex had installed, we stepped off on black and grey marble flooring. "As you can see, there are four restrooms, two for ladies two for men. The ladies will have an attendant to keep the bathroom clean, make sure there's toilet paper, paper towels and sanitary items if needed." Impressed, my brow rose; 'cause I could definitely relate when that time of the month unexpectedly pops up and the sanitary dispensers empty or doesn't work at all. Eight stalls instead of three and all appeared roomy. Then down the hall and into a huge room with grey circular couches on one side, a horseshoe shaped bar stocked with some shit I ain't neva heard of before, to a huge dancefloor with mirrors on the ceilin'. "This is the reggae floor, catering to lovers of reggae music past and present. Let me show you the rest." We actually took the stairs down a level where it was the same set up, but the furniture was cream and the dancefloor held flashin' lights. "This is our pop music floor dependin' on the crowd. Twice a month we'll do house music." Stunned, I followed Hex back to the main floor. "This of course will be R&B and rap. What'd you think?" "Nice very nice," Hex cheesed like he needed validation from me. "Great! Did you have any questions?" "Nope." I told him, eyes still checkin' things out. "Good, good. So as I said Hexagon opens in two days, you ready?" "Yep, I'll be here ready to get shit poppin'. You just have my money come end of the night." Chucklin' Hex stepped closer and whispered, "I'll have it, and anything else you need; and if I don't, I'll get it, just say the word." Brow furrowed, I stared at dis nigga like chile please. "Okay, well get a Tic Tac. Get cho ass out my damn space, cause you ain't gone ever get dese snacks." Slappin' that fake ass contract in his chest, I sauntered over to the bar and ordered a Paul and Coke. *

CHAPTER 10

I must admit, yo girl Tay' was lookin' right if I do say so myself; muah. I blew the mirror a kiss, checked out the goods and smiled, I'd gotten a fresh roller wrap, had dis chick at the mall hook up my face and wore a black and red, skintight Bodycon dress with black and red stilettos; perfection. I'd invited Glenda, Dove and my cousins China, Robin and anyone else I could think of. I was friends wit' radio DJ Amor who worked outta New Haven, and he'd been announcin' Hexagon's openin' every hour. I even had small flyers made, gave a stack to Adam and paid a few kids to stick 'em under car windshields. Hex had given me a blue Honda Civic to get around in and had paid for my outfit. As long as his ass didn't deduct any money from my paycheck, shit was cool. Rollin' up at eleven, I saw a long ass line that damn near stretched the two blocks that made up the club. A male and female bouncer stood at the door, pattin' down bodies and checkin' purses. I parked, checked tha face, stepped out tha car and strutted towards the entrance when I noticed dude turnin' chicks away. The fuck!? Askin' them to wait, I marched up, jostlin' mafuckas, got right in his face and hoped he focused on only one of me as his eyes ping ponged around in their sockets. "Yo, yo! Back of the line. You cute and all but wait cho turn; plus, you in the wrong line sexy." He drawled, showin' a mouthful of capped teeth, "Why are you turnin' women away? Is it full inside already?" dude chuckled. "You hear dis chick Briana? Uh, last I checked my boss' name is Hex; but if you need to be bossed, I can help you once the club closes." The switch jiggled, cause I'm tryina keep it classy and ladylike, but googly eyes was pushin' it. "Nah we ain't full, but no ugly hoes allowed." he burst into laughter. Soundin' like a damn hyena, now that I'm thinkin' 'bout it, he kinda favors one too. Smirk. "Look, either let these ladies in or find yourself another job." Flaggin' the five ladies forward, I waited to see how hyena was gonna play it. "Fuck outta here. I let in who I want. Matter fact, you and these beastly bitches beat it." He snapped. "Okay." Turnin', I pulled out my cell and dialed Hex who answered on the second ring. "Sup Tay' you here yet?" Music played in the background. Hex barked out an order, then resumed conversation with me. "Yep, I'm out front. There's a problem, can you come out here?" "On my way." before I could count to six, Hex strode out wearin' a cream suit and tan Ferragamos on his feet. "Sup Tay', what's the problem?" Dude saw me and Hex talkin' and immediately started sweatin', fidgetin' and shit. Smirk in place, I eagerly ran down hyena's antics with turnin' women away that weren't up to his standards and how he'd also turned all dis fineness away as well. I swear, when Hex turned and looked at hyena, I swear I smelt shit on the night air. "Smitty, I did yo brother Adam a favor givin' you a shot since you fresh out tha joint. You're fired, hit tha road, I'll find someone to stand here. Adam will have your check for.." Hex checked the time on his watch. "...two and a half hours.", then turned to the women Smitty had turned away. "Please accept my apology for the misunderstanding tonight. If you ladies will please follow me, I'll escort you over to VIP. Tonight everything's on the house." Two of the women giggled, one batted her lashes so hard one almost dislodged and flew away. *

"Hey now!" Sang Glenda as she and Dove entered Hexagon; hips shimmyin' to the sounds of Trey Songz 'Slow Motion'. "I like dis shit; classy, upscale and plenty of vics..I mean men." said Dove; eye's eagerly scannin' everythin'. "Good evenin' ladies", both turned, saw me and squealed with excitement. "Tay'! Oh my God you lookin' fly as usual." gushed Glenda, while I peeped Dove smack glossed lips. Whateva boo, I gets full offa da hate huntie. It keeps me fit and trim, so you raggedy bitches can keep hatin'. "Yeah you look nice." Dove grudgingly threw out like I needed her input, NOT! Anyhoo, bein' the good friend I am, I led them over to VIP, set 'em up wit' bottles of Paul and Patron and got to work. * A few drinks, a few dances, coupla words on the mic and I had Hexagon's club goers eatin' out the palm of my hand. Dats what I do boo; give 'em a glimpse of paradise, get 'em droolin', make tha dick hard, now they're comin' out their pockets; tryina impress in hopes of takin' me home. Sorry, tricks are for tha lame, greedy, desperate and of course, tha show offs. I'm just sayin'. * $2500 hundred after a night promotin' wasn't a bad haul, I didn't have to fuck in onea dem nice ass stalls; even though I wouldn't have minded, cause baby, ump, getting' it smackin' in a stall is all that. Bent ova, hands on the seat, foot up on the wall; gotdamn! Biscuits and gravy, my pussy meowin'; down girl, down. Anyhoo, I step outside, mafuckas are everywhere still tryina keep the party goin'. Please. Parkin' lot pimpin's so eighties. Struttin' to my ride, ignorin' whistles and catcalls; 'Cause I'ma fuckin' lady. Step to me, let me see whatchu workin' wit' or shut da hell up. I'm just sayin'. "Fuck you then, yo old ass needa be home suckin' on Geritol!" Some dude yelled, not sure who said it. I pulled out car keys, noticed three dudes standin' beside two bikes parked next to me and rolled my eyes; cause three minus two bikes means someone's a damn passenger. "Man fuck her, pussy probably fulla grey hairs and cobwebs!" said another, all loud before bumpin' fists. The switch jiggled.

Openin' my car door, I threw in my purse but not before grabbin' brass knuckles. "Whas the matter boo? You still mad cause I dissed yo fake ass in tha club? Sittin' there parlayin' while sippin' seltzer water; you'll never be more than whatchu are..a lackey..a yes boy. And sure I might be old boo, but I look damn good, smell good, feel even better. Dis old pussy'll have you on yo knees boo, settin' up yo boys; so don't come for me, cause I'll send you home cryin' to momma." I bossed, battin' eyes and puckering lips. His boys laughed and started clownin' his ass. "Fuck outta here! Fuck all ya'll. Dis dick'll leave her old ass on child..I mean life support." He snapped, makin' his boys laugh harder. Aww poor thangs confused. I stepped up invadin' dudes space, getting' a good look at the whole package. Big feet, big hands, big head, big mouth, grabbin' baggy jeans waistband; I dove inside boxers and felt. Absolutely nothin', even tha nigga balls were undergrown. Felt like I was fingerin' a soggy ass sandwich. I'm just sayin'. "Ump, damn boo, no wonder you mad. Yo ass frustrated. Workin' wit' four inches I can see why, buy a pump boo. Swallow a box of Extenze hunny, cause that right there ain't even a snack in my book. I'd gobble yo shit and still have room for more." Withdrawin' my hand, I gave my fingers a sniff, then sucked 'em dry. "Ump, just like I thought. Here I am fondlin' yo kids toy and ain't no excitement goin' on. No pre-cum, youse a dry fuck boo..goodnight." Wide smirk in place, I gave his ass a second to let it digest, turned and switched back to my car. * "So that's why you kept sexy dude to yo self, you ain't want this competition 'cause I would've shut shit downn!" exclaimed Dove's ole loud behind. Eyin' her ensemble of faded sweatpants, holey tee shirt, dirty scarf and run over sneakers, I couldn't do nothin' but laugh. Chile please, wake up from that coma you in cause that shit would NEVER fuckin' happen, even on my worse damn day, okay. "You really think so hunh? Well Hex's hirin' down at his strip club, why don't you trot down there, flash some thigh and see whatchu can reel in." Dove twisted her lips. "Why I gotta strip? Yo old ass ain't strippin'?" She retorted. Dis bitch right here. Its Sunday, I'm tryina chill, listen to some oldies and sip a lil liquor and here her ass comes irkin' my damn nerves. "Listen Dove.....can you hear me or are yo ears as dirty and useless as that outfit you sportin'? If you feel like you wanna promote for Hex then by all means do so. I don't control what Hex does and says, go for yours boo. If you're waitin' on me to speak for yo ass, you'll sprout balls and shoot sperm. Now let this be the last damn time you swell all up over a damn nigga, who by the way I ain't fuckin', have never fucked and have no intentions on fuckin'...clear?" Dove stared for a second, like shit ain't compute, before she smirked and poured herself a drink. "Damn gurl, why so hostile? I thought we supposed to be tight, like Super Glue. I ask one lil question and you flip." Now I eyed her ass back. Jealousy's such an ugly thing, and lookin' at her I could tell it had taken root and festered. Poor thang really wants to be me out here, her ass fienin'. I wonder if I told her suck my toes, lick my scalp, how fast would her ass move. Smirk. "Girl you know we cool. I'm just lettin' you know, go for yours." Ooo, tha bitch phoniness rubbin' off! "Maybe I will." "Change yo clothes first. You don't wanna be confused wit' a homeless can collector." Bam! *

CHAPTER 11

Fed up with Taylor's comin' for her and always thinkin' she's better than everyone else, Dove stared at her pill bottles sittin' atop her kitchen table; debatin' on how many to drop in Taylor's drink. It was time for a lil payback, sleepin' with Kione had been a bust as Taylor barely spared him a glance upon seein' him at her place. Once Taylor was knocked out was the dilemma. What to do? Her plan to have Taylor sellin' ass was still on the menu, but she needed money to get shit started. Standing, Dove strode down the hall and back into her bathroom, snatched open the medicine cabinet and grabbed a bottle of Senokot. An evil smile formed.. * "I'm glad we're back doin' these parties 'cause I need tha money." said Glenda, puttin' the finishin' touches on a bowl of potato salad. "I know that's right, I started to do it at my place, but most of the party goers live here and don't have cars." said Dove. "It's cool. Like I said, I can use tha money." "And Marcus won't mind?" Asked Dove, not really caring as long as she got what she wanted. "Nah, Marcus and I don't live together, plus he's out of town visitin' his parents down in Florida." "Whateva. What else you cook?" Glenda smacked her lips. "Yo ass ain't kick in, so don't worry 'bout all that." she sharply spat. "Whoa!" Innocent look in place, Dove threw up her hands. "What's with the animosity? I'm just askin' damn!" "Whateva." Glenda threw back, turned to the stove and flipped over the middle finger, twice. "Okay, I told everyone it starts around one, so they'll be good; and saucy and good and horny upon arrival." Glenda nodded in approval. "Good, is Taylor comin'?" Hatred flashed, then was quickly gone upon Dove's face. "As far as I know." Checkin' tha time, Dove stood. "I'll make the drinks and punch so you'll have time to shower." volunteered Dove while watchin' Glenda. "Okay, thanks." Glenda took the chicken out, drained it on paper towels and said, "It's eleven forty-five, I'm gonna go shower and get ready." Dove watched her leave, waited a beat, then quickly made a pitcher of punch, spiked with Vodka, threw in some cherries and lemons. Grabbed Taylor's Paul, opened it, then poured in the whole bottle of Senokot. * Once again, Glenda's house was packed with the young, hot and horny. Jim Jones loudly blared about 'Balling' as bodies dry humped on the couch, grinded against the wall, fingerin' on the stairs. Liquor flowed, blunts were lit, E pills swallowed and mollies sniffed, getting' everyone in tha mood for tha main event. * Bored, I decided to troop it over to Glenda and Dove's fuck fest, maybe I'd get lucky and find some ding a ling to play wit'. Damn, I remember that song, Chucklin' I strode past Rosalie's surprised to see her place dark. Knowin' how they got down, I wouldn't be surprised if they had their own orgy goin' on. Openin' tha screen, I twisted the door knob and stepped inside, nose immediately wrinklin' from the smell of rank pus', sour balls and ass. Smelled like shit on a cracker, I'm just sayin'. Closin' tha door, I gave a look around, takin' in tha fuckery goin' on. Dove hid behind a speaker recordin' Hartford's previous Attorney General gettin' her twat eaten by Glenda, while Rosalie suckled like a newborn on her breasts. Right beside the coffee table lay Toni, gettin' pounded from the back so hard her tits were slappin' her chin. On the other couch sat Brick bein' pleasured by Shelly's crack head ass; thick globs of slob coatin' his shaft. Walkin' into the kitchen, I opened the fridge and grabbed my drank, already prepared and reat to go just how I like it. Takin' a sip, I snatched a piece of chicken and started up the stairs just to be nosy; feel me. Upstairs fuck sounds were goin' off left and right; that shit kinda turned me on. Nipples hard, I hit tha bathroom door, clunkin' Kione who lay on his back in tha head, Kelly atop him gettin' her bounce on. Lips curled in distaste, I started to slam his melon a few times, leave his ass wit' a few speed knots and a helluva headache. Instead I turned and walked away. In the bedroom..hot damn, new meat! My eyes slid over creamy chocolate skin, firm ass cheeks flexin' as he pounded some chick I've neva seen before. When he threw legs on shoulders I ain't give a hoot who her ass was, I wanted what she had, fuck tha dumb shit. Strollin' up on tha bed, I ran a hand up his back, then gasped in surprise. Hex! Stumblin' back, I dropped my drink and hauled ass out tha room, down tha stairs and out tha door so fast I came out my damn shoe. * Fuck was Hex doin' there? What kinda of fuckery was Dove stirrin' up? I knew it was her idea, 'cause Glenda had never seen Hex and only knew of him through conversation. "Ooo, dis trick done flipped tha switch, wait til' I see that tramp." I spat while pacin'. And anotha thing, why tha hell my stomach rollin', pitchin' and grumblin' like I gotta take a mean ass shit? I've eaten Glenda's food on numerous occasions and never had no problems. Racin' to tha toilet I made it just in time as everythin' I've eaten came pourin' out like runnin' water. Ooo, me and my asshole both on fire, sure as I love to suck a dick and gargle cum. I know ole sneaky ass Dove did this shit. Poott..xcuse me...but soon as I get off dis toilet, I'ma drag that hoe. * An hour later, showered, dressed and Pepto coatin' my stomach and sneaks laced up tight, I stomped my way over to Glenda's and marched inside; eyes on patrol for Dove's ass. Glenda ran up, worried look plastered on her face.

"What's wrong Tay'? You look pissed off and ready to kill." Ump, you damn right! "Let me ask you somethin'," I stepped so close nipples were damn near touchin', "who made all the dranks tonight?" Confusion colored her face, not that I gave a damn cause both of 'em can get tha beat down. "Dove made 'em. I told her not to make yours too strong. She offered 'cause it was gettin' late and I still had to get dressed. Why? What's the matter?" Ignorin' all dat extra babblin' she was doin', I started up the stairs, jumpin' over a pair of panties so soiled and crunchy I know them joints walked on their own. Ump, whoever they belonged to pus' probably reeked of onions, ammonia and hot garbage. I'm just sayin'. I guess Glenda knew not to follow cause when I hit tha top, her ass was nowhere in sight. The bathroom door stood wide open, but was empty. Comin' to a closed bedroom door, I halted. Earlier Dove and Hex had been inside, cockin' ear to wood I gave a listen, heard nothin' and hoped her ass was sleep when I burst in and if Hex was still wit' her, his ass could have a kick to tha balls if he tried to stop me. Turnin' tha knob I swung that door open so hard, the knob put a dent in the wall and there she was; ass up, face down, lips wrapped around Brick's monster. Jeez Louise, this niggas penis sure got around! Neither of their asses paid me any mind, Brick too busy yellin' and tryin' to stuff his whole body between her jaws. Grim smile in place, four steps and her weave was wrapped around my wrist, my left came up and started whalin' on her face, that's right, a leftie. Neva sleep on us boo, 'cause we'll lay a mafucka out wit' one punch; 'cause yo dumb ass lookin' fo' the right. Blood shot out her nose and dribbled from her mouth. One eye was already swellin' closed when tha dirty skank leaned in and bit my titty! Fuck they do that at?! Okay, she wanna get greasy and take it there, then let's go! I drug her ass off tha dick with a nasty suckin' sound and muttered, "Get yoself checked boo." to Brick and watched his eyes widen before mines swung back on Dove who was scratchin' tha shit outta my hand in an effort to get free. Not! Raisin' a sneakered foot, I kicked her ass smack in tha chest. "Yo chill Taylor. You wanna rumble, throw the fair one, don't sneak her." said Brick. Please. Did dis ninja really think this chick had wins against me in a fair one? That used up, no walls havin' hoe done brainwashed Brick wit' tha pussy. Yankin' my hand free, I tore out a clump of glued in weave, tossed it in her face and backed up. "You heard him hoe, get yo jealous ass up and run me tha one." Dazed and confused, this trick rose to her feet acceptin' tha challenge. poor thangs 'bout to get embarrassed in front of Brick. Crackin' knuckles, I waited. Dove spat a wad of blood, then gave a bloody tooth smile. "Wass tha matta," she mumbled through puffy lips. "stomachache?" My smile appeared. "Nope, but yours will in about three minutes." I taunted. "Bitch please, you've always been jealous of me Tay'.

I'm everythin' you're not, young, pretty, popular with the men, young." Ooo, I'm done talkin', it's on and crackin'. I'm sorry for tearin' up yo shit Glenda, but I gots to fuck dis hootchie up! "Run up then witcho young ass. You should have no problem beatin' dis old freak down to tha gristle." Dove screamed, ran up and swung, catchin' me dead in tha nose, blood immediately gushed warm and salty over my lips. I came back wit' a four piece, cause that's what I do; hittin' her twice in one eye and one to her nose, causin' her to yelp in pain and tha otha dead in her big ass mouth. Brick yelled somethin' and I vaguely heard tha music lower and feet poundin' up the stairs. "Oh snap!" A high pitched voice yelled out. "Five hundred on Taylor, dat old bitch a beast wit' dem hands!" "Fuck outta here! She like sixty out chere ha ass gonna run outta steam! I bet a G!" Screamed another. Dove swung a barefoot, catchin' me in tha knee, it stung, but cause she's barefoot I knew it hurt her ass more than me. The same knee she kicked knocked all wind from her stomach, then I did it three more times and jumped back when throw up came up and out all over Glenda's carpet. I tagged her twice more, all body shots; came wit' an uppercut and watched as she slipped and fell in her throw up. Bouncin' round like Muhammad Ali, I started talkin' junk. "Aww, tummy ache? Maybe you ate somethin' that turned yo stomach." punch to tha back. Frustrated, Dove started kickin' and windmillin' to keep me away. Hunny do yo homework before comin' to class cause you 'bout to fail, big time. I'm just sayin'. Niggas were shoutin' for her to get up, to let me let her up. I know you shouldn't play wit' yo food, but I couldn't help it. Besides, I was still pissed, so I eased up, givin' her a chance to get it together. Usin' tha bed, Dove pulled herself back up, turned and met my bitch/pimp slap full force. Dudes were oohin', cursin' and yellin' for her to shake shit off while still others were yellin' it's over stay down. "Ready?" I asked, wonderin' if her ass could even see me wit' one eye that was half open. Let me help her not see at all; say goodnight Gracie, sorry showin' my age. Dove swung, I ducked, chopped her in tha throat, stomped her foot and when she slightly bent, anotha uppercut that clicked teeth to tongue, a shot to the eye and down she went, face first in throw up that looked like cum stew. Nasty slore. *

CHAPTER 12

Hex's strip club was off the chain! Big ass gilded cages hung from the ceilin' with chicks covered in body paint that glowed in the dark. Carpet up in VIP, two bars, comfy swivel chairs, a huge stage with two poles, mirrors etc. In the back, big dressin' room with lockers and even some stripper gear for those unprepared, and of course six private rooms for those willin' to shell out the cash. I eyed a cute ass DJ settin' up equipment, this one looked a lot better than the other who worked at Hex's nightclub. Hmm, I could use a snack. It had been five days since my fight with Dove, afterwards I walked off wit' $1200 hundred after I made they asses share the wealth. Hell, they wouldn't have won without me. Anyhoo, some manly lookin' shim ran the bar, caught her ass eyin' alla this but no thanks, I don't need no more stalkers in my life okay. Hex appeared like he was camera watchin', awaitin' my arrival. "Glad

you made it, ready to work?" He asked. "Boo I'm always ready."
Ask 'bout me boo. Hex turned, walked over to the DJ and
introduced us, "Corey, Taylor; Taylor, Corey."; explained what
I'd be doin' and left me to it. And hot damn! Pussy on tha griddle
ole Corey had it goin' on! Now I've had my share of man meat,
but baby; I was ready to strip naked jump on the ones and twos
and get busy! He stood at least six feet; ump I like 'em tall. Excuse
me, I drooled a lil; cocoa colored skin, thick brows, long lashes,
slightly upturned nose, thin stashe, and full pussy eatin' lips,
gawd! "Nice to meet you Taylor." pearly whites flashed. Did he
just say he wanted to eat me? Hmp, he put Idris Elba, my man
crush, on the back burner. Yess lawd I done found me a new toy
and as long as he had seven or better, we could do business.*
Comin' in wit' groceries, I run into Glenda, who still looked
pissed off. Oh well boo, stop hangin' wit' rachet hoes that always
keep shit goin' and you'll be fine. I'm just sayin'. "That was
fucked up Tay'." she said, pout on her lips. "Girl what are you
ramblin' 'bout? Grab those bags and c'mon in." Doin' as told,
Glenda carried three bags inside, followed me in the kitchen and
took a seat. "Fightin' Dove in my son's room, that was dead
wrong. You tore up all his shit." I snorted, cause that raggedy ass
Salvation Army shit was f'd up fo' she put it on tha truck and
took it home. "Yeah, sorry 'bout dat, but Dove's ass was askin'
for it; so I had to deliver." Glenda frowned. "Why didn't you

drag her outside Tay'? I mean, I would've never disrespected yo place like that." Cause yo ass would've caught two in the chops hunny. "Fine Glenda. I said I was sorry and as a show of faith I'll replace tha bed, TV and dresser okay." Glenda smiled, jumped up and hugged me. "Thank you. Now why were you two fightin'?" Cause Dove's a hatin' ass, jealous slore; her ass needs a refill on her crazy meds, I'm sure she doesn't take. "Did you ask Dove?" "Nope, didn't get the chance. After you beat her up, Rick and 'nem ranked her up so bad she ran cryin' from my place." retorted Glenda. I laughed so hard I caught a cramp in my side. Whoo, that Dove, what a character. "C'mon, ya'll tore up my shit, at least tell me why Tay'." Omg! If she didn't stop fuckin' whinin'! Groceries put away, my cell rang. Glancin' at the screen I saw Brandon callin'..again. Had I not made myself clear at the grocery store? "Hol' on Glenda." Pushin' talk I snarled, "Fuck nucca, are you retarded?! Didn't I tell yo ass to stop blowin' me up if you ain't got no damn money!" "I have $2500 hundred, now get off your ass and come see me. I'm at the Hilton downtown." Brandon rolled off, but I ain't feelin' how he's comin' at a bitch; so Taylor James ain't goin' no damn where. "Okay lover." I purred. "I'll be there round midnight." then hung up on his still ramblin' ass. "Girl, you stay wit' all tha men blowin' you up." "And you know dis. Can I help it if all the men wanna come in my yard?" I did a lil hip shimmey, then took

a seat. "I beat Dove's ass cause tha tramp admitted puttin' somethin' in my drink that caused tha shits." Glenda's eyes ballooned. "No shit..uh, you know what I mean." she quickly amended, her ass better had cause the switch will flip and pow! *
"Aargh!" Screamed Dove, then did it again so loud her throat itched. Her upstairs neighbor stomped on her floor causin' plaster chips to fall from the ceilin' and coat the scarf Dove wore. "Fuckin' Taylor's dead!" Pacin', Dove scratched a bald spot through her scarf and cursed again. Nothin' she did seemed to bring that hoe down a peg and show her selfish self that she wasn't the only one who could get it. Hex had given her a job waitin' tables at both spots but dudes were stingy wit' uppin' tips, expectin' an ass squeeze and shit. Fuck, she might as well strip and make big money. A smile bloomed. Hell yeah, thought Dove, she could make enough to get her plan up and runnin' and bring Tay's ass down. *

CHAPTER 13

Whoo hoo! Reggae weeks here bitches! I loved me some reggae week, ump! Dem sexy, heavy accent, illegal bastards can get it! Just gotta be careful, some of 'em crazier than a loony escapee from lockup. I'm just sayin'. Ty and Omaire were buggin' a bitch on that ring status. Yeah Ty talked a good one, but he missed these cookies and milk, ya heard. Anyway, fuck them I'm out here! Today was the Jamaican Parade and I can't wait to see what delicacies stroll past shirtless, sweaty and lookin' good. Hot damn, let's go! From Main and Albany down to Main and Tower was blocked off and I planned to trek that long shit, which ended at the West Indian club; which would be bangin' tonight. Red eeny meeny shorts, black and red sandals, a red half shirt and mirrored shades on, I stepped on the scene; head boppin' to Popcaan blastin' from some huge ass speakers. Aww shit! Corey! He nodded, then jumped off the back. I swear tha dick kept jumpin' as he walked towards me lookin' good and smellin' right. "Sup Taylor, you lookin' good, I didn't know you did the Jamaican Parade." "Yep, I can take care of myself, I ain't worried about the few hood boogers down here." "I hear that, come ride the float for a sec." I smiled, got my switch on and jumped on that shit; and when Notch's 'Nuttin A Go So' came on, my hips started winin'. I broke out in tha butterfly, then backed it up on Corey's sexy ass, cheesin' while posin'; hatin' hoes face's green wit' envy. * I jumped off Corey's float down on Westland and Main. 'Cause I ain't tryin' to sample just one, you ain't know. Dudes are like Lay's chips, Taylor can't eat just one! Ooo chile, all flavored M&M's were strollin' round, some wit' their chicks, some without; like that'd stop me. Ump, I love sweets boo, watch me work. Dis light bright, shirtless, dreads to his waist, eye patch wearin', sexy mofo strolled past wit' some chick I barely spared a glance. Steppin' up, I blocked sexy's path, eyed him up and down, licked my lips, passed my number and kept walkin'; ignorin' that hoe who was wildin' talkin' 'bout, "Jayshon who da fuck is she!" Hol' on a sec, and you'll find out when Jayshon ain't nowhere to be found boo. I'm just sayin'. By the time I reached Tower, I was feelin' good off a pint of Paul, a Corona and an E pill. I was approached by a few possibles; but don't be desperate boo, tellin' me whatchu gonna do to me. Shit like, 'Girl I'll suck yo pussy from tha back while standin' on my head.'; only to buss yo ass cause yo ass failed dat shit in gym class, while yo tongue feels like a soggy ass washrag. Or 'Girl I'll have yo ass searchin' fo' me wit' a flashlight.'. Please, yo flashlight need batteries, and yo fuck game needs immediate CPR, fuck outta here! I'm just sayin'. Anyhoo, a bitch had to damn near elbow a hoe in tha throat to get through tha crowd n shit. Damn, let greatness through when you see it. My eyes widened, three chicks were dancin' in tha middle of tha street, a few greenbacks strewn at their feet. Ump, chump change. Let me show dese youngins a lil' somethin'. Smile wide, juices flowin'. I started wit' a lil Skip to ma lou, that got the three's attention, along wit' tha crowd; so I hit tha Pon di river, did the Bike Back and when I saw my pile growin' and them chicks hatin', it was on! Bogle, I did that; Skankin', owned it! I even threw in a lil of QQ's moves. When it was all said and done, I had to knock some jafakin' out, 'cause she claimed I stole her pile of money. Yeah I did, annddd what!? * The Wes' was packed! I couldn't walk without bumpin' some damn body. Some yeah, the shit was on purpose, I'm just sayin'. These strong, muscular arms encircled my waist as I stood at tha bar. Ooo, what's that I'm feelin'..a mafuckin' kielbasa! Ooo kitty meowin', scratchin' thong. Turnin' I smiled, Corey! I ain't lost my touch, ole girl can still sniff out a footlong! "Hey boo, how you doin'?" Corey lookin' all serious, leaned in, gripped my earlobe, nibbled, then whispered, "Who you here wit' ma?" Ooo, dis ninja gonna make me do him right gotdamn it! Good thing I had a spare thong in my purse, cause tha one I wore was d-o-n-e! Ump, dis ninja got some moves. Ooo, I can't wait to ride that candy stick. "Whatchu drinkin' ma?" "Paul and Coke." I answered still grindin' on that beef. Corey paid for my drink, got himself a bottled water and said, "Wanna dance?" Sheeit, do birds poop on windshields!? Hell to tha yess! Fuck wit' me, I'll hike my leg on the dancefloor, push my soaked thong to the side and serve his ass somethin' he'll never forget. Three dances later, Corey and I strolled out back where grills were goin'. Tables and chairs were set up so people could get their grub on; from choices like, stamp and go, callaloo fritters, ox tails with pigeon peas and rice and steamed fish to name a few. I had a damn ball! Got a rack of numbers and decided to go home, alone. * Glenda and I were chillin' outside wit' Rosalie when who pulls up, Dove. Smirk on my face, I watched that bitch like a hawk as she stepped from her bucket, only for my jaw to drop when a pink replica of the car I saw at Joshua's pulled up behind Dove. "That's a nice car." said Rosalie. The door opened and out stepped a thin, Hispanic who started in our direction. "Sup ya'll." greeted Dove. I ain't pay her ass no mind as dude walked up askin' for me. Fuck? I don't know dis ninja. "That would be me." without a word, he handed over a set of car keys. "The cars from Joshua. He's currently in Atlanta and asks that you call him this evening at seven." Turnin', he walked away and flagged down an approaching taxi. "Damn Tay'! Go! A car?! Who's Joshua and does he have a brother?" Dove sarcastically lashed out, like she wanted a rematch. "Appears so, you see it parked right behind yo buck..I mean car and I don't know if dude has a brother. I never asked." I could hear her teeth grindin' which tickled the hell outta me. Poor tink tink. "C'mon Glenda, lets take a spin." Glenda jumped up, while Rosalie sat steamin' in her seat. Tunafish better stay seated. "I'm comin' too." Dove called out, already on my heels like a stray mongrel lookin' for a treat. Ump, that fit Dove's ass to a T. Anyhoo, I let Dove's ass tag along after fiddlin' wit' seats, mirrors and music. Pullin' off Nelson Street, I turned on Main and got my cruise on. When I hit tha Ave I pulled up in Micky D's got in tha drive thru and mentally smiled 'cause Joshua deserved tha full treatment. maybe an impromptu trip to the ATL was in order. * "Thank you Joshua, I love the car." was my greetin' when Joshua finally answered. "You're welcome. So how've you been?" He asked. Fuck you think, gooder then a mug, cause I'm ridin' too cute. "Very well thank you for askin' and you, how're you doin'?" That's right I know how to put on my white girl voice. I'ma jack of all trades boo. We ended up talkin' two hours before I fell asleep on Josh's borin' ass. * The next day I copped a round trip ticket off Priceline to Atlanta, packed a few slutty pieces of sleep wear, among other shit, texted Glenda to keep an eye on my place, jumped in my car and headed towards Bradley International Airport. * Man mafuckas that worked airport security needed a swift kick in tha damn balls! Give a nucca a uniform and a lil power and they lose they rabbit ass mind. I almost missed my fuckin' flight cause some fat, nasty, sweatin' under AC bastard decided I had to walk tha green mile. First, the metal detector, that shit ain't make a peep, so fatty sends me through this x-ray machine where his greedy ass can see what I ate lastnight. Then he claims I need to be body searched 'cause I look suspicious! Ooo tha switch was jigglin', only reason I ain't spaz cause I ain't need his fat ass claimin' I threatened him, but if I miss my flight all bets are off. * Forty minutes later, pissed and in the air, I ordered a Bacardi and Pepsi and tried to calm down cause I ain't wanna go off on Joshua when I landed. Some blonde chick sittin' next to me was snorin' and slobberin', so I slapped in headphones and pulled up tha music on my phone. 'House' by Rico Love played immediately changin' my mood. * Hartsfield-Jackson airport was big as hell. By the time I found the exit I was aggravated all over again; and when I stepped outside, only to be blasted wit' one hundred and five degrees of dry heat wit' no breeze in sight, I knew for the next three days AC would be my best damn friend. * The Ritz Carlton hotel was pretty damn snazzy, they even had their own damn magazine!

After checkin' in and flirtin' wit' a pimply faced kid who carried my luggage, his ass cheesed showin' off a rack of braces. All he needed were some taped up frames and he could star in one a them nerd flicks. Turnin' the AC up, I tipped Deon tha nerd and flopped on the king sized, soft as cotton mattress. Joshua would be tied up for tha next three and a half hours, nap time. * Ooo chile, the Ritz was doin' me right gotdamnit! Marble floorin', a bachelor's chest fulla booze and snacks, marble bath with granite vanity and rain shower head and Italian frette linen. That's the good shit right there, and ma-fuck-in butler services. Ump, Joshua ain't know it yet, but he'd be pickin' up my tab, 'cause momma planned on usin everythin' in here! Takin' a shower, dem fluffy ass Ritz towels soaked up water wit' one damn pat on skin. Whoo, let me get dressed fo' dis room cause an orgasm. * Downstairs, I asked Deon to let me know when Dr. Joshua Browne arrived; that I was his fiancée and was here to surprise him. Then I strolled around the huge lobby registration area, and noticed a few placards on fine dinin' areas. There were quite a few, but since I had to leave AC to go, they were immediately disqualified. The Atlanta grill it is! "He just pulled up Ms. James." Heart racin', I almost cut Deon's ass for sneakin' up on me like that. "Thanks hon'." A fiver changed hands, as I Top Model walked across tha floor, catchin' Joshua just as the doors slid smoothly open and he stepped inside; eyes widenin' in pleasure as I knew they would, 'cause they all do. "Taylor!" Warm hug. "What a nice surprise, what are you doin' here?" "Surprise! After receivin' yo wonderful gift I had to come thank you personally." Leanin' in, I softly pecked his lips. I might put lips and tongue to work in other places, but kissin' is personal boo, although I do make exceptions. "I hope you're hungry, I figured we can dine in, get to know each other a lil better.." Pause. "... unless you're tired?" He did look a lil worn round the edges, still kinda cute though. "Uh sure, sure, we can have dinner over at Atlanta Grill. I hear their foods really good." "Lead tha way handsome." I purred, then held his hand. I think I read somewhere that whites were more affectionate out in public. The Grill had inside and outside dinin', Josh selected out, which had my lips curlin'. Who wanted to eat when they're hotter than tha food on the plate? But I didn't complain, yet. It wasn't bad, evenin' had fell, so it was slightly cooler and every now and then a lil breeze blew through. "Good evening and welcome to the Atlanta Grill, my name is Nathan and I'll be your server this evening. May I start you off with a drink and some of our delicious appetizers?" Sheeit, I had my menu open before my ass hit tha seat. I'm hungry and ready to grub, plus I had to hide tha smile and laughter bubblin' to tha surface. Nathan was built like the terminator guy, looked like that Fabio boy and sounded like Mike Tyson, hilarious! Back under control, menu lowered, I replied, "Yes, I'll have the crab cake appetizer, the spring mountain half chicken with a side of collards." "And you sir?" "Yes, I'll have the grilled salad, and the redfish with a side of grilled broccolini." Nathan smiled. "Wonderful choices and your beverages?" "I'll take a Sprite." "I'll have a lemon water." said Joshua. Nathan thanked us again for choosin' to dine at Atlanta Grill and disappeared. Joshua chuckled, eyes alit with humor. "What's so funny?" "Nathan, I wasn't expectin' such a high voice to come from such a big guy." We laughed. "I'm glad you came Taylor. I was beginning to think you weren't interested." Never that boo, the request lines long. I woulda got to you eventually, but that ride sure moved you on up. "I'm interested Josh, its just you're a very busy man and very hard to reach. But, I'm here now, so tell me all about Joshua." Durin' tha course of his blabbin', I learned he's been engaged but neva married; his fiancée was killed on a skiing trip, her ass was hit by a damn elk, probably was racin' to get away from all that inane chatter flowin'. He had no kids but wanted at least six. Next! Cause I don't want shit to do wit' Keone's ass, fuck I look like poopin' out five more? Dis ninja done sniffed too many Pampers or sumthin'. Our appetizers arrived and baby, them crab cakes were slap somebody momma good! Josh asked about me, so I gave him a lil info. Shit like, my age, how I ain't want no damn kids and how peaceful I was wit' myself, yawn! The main course arrived and I tore that chicken and collards downn! Chile I was scrapin' up tha plate, swipin' juices up with my finger and suckin' it off down to tha knuckle. Ain't no shame over here boo. Full as fuck, I still ate a slice of chocolate peanut butter mousse cake and took a bite of Josh's chocolate moo cake. * After dinner, we took a quick stroll through somethin' called Chilli Gardens or some shit like that; borin'! I wanted to party, not stroll through bullshit ass shrubbery cut in strange shapes dotted wit' ugly statues. "Would you like to go dancin'?" Hell yeah! But a bitch ain't tryina be fox trottin' and doin' tha waltz. No smank you! "Sure, that's if you're not too tired." What I really thought was, by myself fool, take yo straitlaced ass on to bed, I got this! "Well," he drawled, "I do have a conference call around eleven. I don't think an hour or two will hurt. C'mon, let's check out Blind Willie's." said Josh, so wit' heavy heart I agreed. * Blind Willie's was a blues, jazz spot. It was cute and all, but definitely not my cup of Paulie, okay. Nick Moss, whoever tha hell he was, had performed the night before. Like I gave two big balls as Josh went on and on about how he wished he'd known. Shit. I wish I knew how borin' yo ass is. I woulda waited til' you came back, hitchu wit' the snap, crackle, pop and bounced on his ass. Even the drink names were wack; a Blues Brothers, BB King on crack, which was hella offensive. I ordered a fuckin' water and clock watched countin' down that hour or two. * That horror over and back at the Ritz, we stepped off the elevator on the eighteenth floor; my mind on puttin' Josh to sleep, changin' clothes and headin' back out. Shit, it wasn't even eleven yet, fuck I look lik goin' to bed like I'm eighty nine in someone's nursing home. Car or not, Joshua's fuck game betta be hittin' or bottom of the list he goes. * Okay, okay I can get into this right here. Josh and I were booty butt naked as he massaged fineness from head to toe. "Hmm that feels good." huskily slid out, hard penis bobbed and weaved across my lower back. I'd snuck a look, seven and a half thick ass inches, passable. "Roll over!" Hell yeah! Rollin' with a wink and spread legs, I waited for dick delivery. Choo choo! Chug on in dis cave boo, so I can rattle yo caboose, I'm just sayin'. Josh trailed kisses down my body, raising goosebumps of anticipation. My legs opened wider, heels hangin' off the bed's edge. Josh dove in, tongue twirlin', swirlin', suckin' and nibblin' on swollen clit, a light blow and ass lifted from mattress, aww sukey, eat it all up boo, get dese snacks. Legs raised, I circled his neck and got my grind on.. *

CHAPTER 14

The club I went to lastnight was bangin'! I woke up this mornin' kinda hung over. Niggas were buyin' me drinks left and right and I was chuggin' 'em, ump. I danced, flirted and served a hand job in the mens room to a cutie who was sellin' dime bags of bud, I got mines for free. Anyhoo, I ordered up room service, a ham, onion and cheese omelet, sausage patty's and hash browns wit' a big ole glass of Pepsi. Full and ready to stroll before I blistered and melted from the heat, I stepped outside in a cute off white babydoll dress, white tie up the calf sandals, black and white purse and my shades restin' atop hair pulled back in a ponytail and hit the streets. In daylight Atlanta was kinda cute and teemin' wit' people goin' to work, shoppin' and just bein' tourists. Best believe I got my tourist on too. The Agatha Mystery Theater, Margaret Mitchell Square, the Candler Building were some of the places I went. Lunch time rolled around so I stopped at a cute lil bistro place called

Juke Joint and had a quick bite, only for the switch to flip when on my fork lay a long strand of blonde hair. Aww hell no! "Waiter! I need a fuckin' waiter right damn now!" Custies nervously eyed me up and down as I banged my glass and kept yellin', "Where's tha mafucka who brought me a plate fulla white girl hair!" A tall, lanky lookin' manager raced over. "Ma'am, please lower your voice, what seems to be the problem?" Dudes tag read Louis, supervisor. "Look here Louis. I'ma grown ass woman, if I wanna get loud then gotdamnit I'll get loud and ain't a damn thang you can do but turn red in tha face, like you're doin'. I ordered a Juke cheeseburger with fried okra and garlic steamed broccoli, not a white girl hair special. Now intseada standin' here jabberin' 'bout tha level of my voice, yo ass needs to be getting' it right, before I stand outside and show all yo custies what you serve up in dis hairy establishment!" Beet red in tha face, Louis comped my meal, gave me a free slice of lemon cheesecake and profusely apologized. I saw a sign for the Georgia Aquarium and decided to go inside, chuckin' tha cheesecake on the way inside; picture me eatin' anythin' else from tha Juke Joint. That place was humongous! From the penguin exhibit to seals, sharks and all kinds of colorful fish. I got my pose on and snapped away. Yess boo, catch all dis if you can. Postin' a few on the Gram, I finished tourin' took a free booklet and bounced. * Josh was ready and waitin' for a sista when I stepped foot back inside tha Ritz, just chillin' in front of my hotel door like a damn stalker! I snorted, cause if Josh turned into another Brandon I'ma whip out tha mace and do him right damn it! "Taylor! Where have you been? I snuck out early to spend time with you, but you weren't in your room, nor answering you phone." Whoa! Hang on one hairy back minute, I know dis seven inch seven minute man ain't questionin' my got-damn-ma-fuckin'-where-bouts! Last I checked, Isabel Janae was restin' in Our Lady Of Sorrows cementary, and my hubby was still in lock-up wit' anotha three to five to go, so don't do me boo, you definitely don't wanna see that side of me. "Uh....are you serious right now?" "Well Taylor, I did gift you with a car." Ohh its throw shit you got me in my face day. "And I gave you pussy and sucked yo pecker." I threw back, switch jigglin' like a mafucka. "There's no need to be vulgar, we're two adults having a conversation. Why don't we continue this in your room?" Arch of brow. "How about you kiss my black ass. That car you gave is just that, a car. Not a license or receipt that you bought and own my ass, so have your lackey come get dat shit fo' I burn it tha fuck up! Lose my number nigga, forget everythin' 'bout me, now watch me walk. See me in yo dreams cause its tha last you'll see of me asshole!" I made sure to slam tha door right in his face. * Fuck stayin', cause all damn night Josh rang both cell and room phones; and from six am deliveries started arrivin'.

Flowers, candy, a singin' telegram, blah, blah, blah; stick if far up yo ass cause I ain't interested, ya heard. Packed up and reat to go, next time I come to this fuckin' city it won't be to see a damn man. I'm comin' to twerk on a lap, tea bag some balls and slob on a dick, then take my ass home. * Back in tha town of shiesty chicks, stick ups and more, I never felt so good. By the time I drove Josh's car home, lanky dude was sittin' at tha curb, big box in hand. Rollin' my eyes I stepped out, walked up, dropped keys beside him and kept it movin'. "Marcus! Can you help me please?" I called out, just as he closed Glenda's door. "Sure." Marcus jogged over and grabbed suitcase and shoppin' bags. "Excuse me. Uhm, I spoke with Josh and he wants you to keep the car and the gift." Marcus and I stared at a box from Harpers Furs. Well damn, I don't own a fur, that shit will look real gangsta on me, bitches would be sick; espically Dove and Rosalie's slutty daughters. Should I? Then I remembered how crazy Josh was actin'. "Hell naw, I don't want nothin' his ass got, now beat it. C'mon Marcus." We strode up to my door, I unlocked it, took my shit, thanked him and stepped inside and closed the door. My cell rang, Joshua. My molars ground together. "What!" I snapped. "didn't I tell yo ass to kick rocks!" "Taylor, please listen. You're right, I had no right to treat or talk to you that way. Please give us another chance, let me make it up to you." I'd set tha phone down a long time ago, so I had no clue what Joshua was sayin', nor did I give a hot shit. I put my things away, jumped in tha shower, dressed in jeans, tee and sneakers, grabbed money, keys and phone and headed out the door, headed over to T-Mobile to change my number. * "Need a ride?" Comin' outta T-Mobile who do I see askin' if I need a ride, Jermaine's undercover behind. Ugh! Could my day get any worse?! "Nah I'm good, thanks though." Hell naw ninja, I don't wanna sit on cummy seats or smell musty balls and sour backed up ass meat, no thanks boo. Jermaine sucked his choppers, probably dislodgin' a bunch of pubic hairs which he swallowed. "Here you go. Yo ass ain't all that Tay', it's just a ride. Ain't nobody gonna kidnap yo ass." Ooo, no he didn't! I know yo ass ain't kidnappin' nothin' right here, wrong sex boo and I don't carry round a damn strap on fo' you to ride on. Bam! "I never said you'd kidnap me, nor do I think I'm all that." I am boo and it's eatin' you up inside ain't it? Hell, if I gave you a shot, would yo meat even get hard? Ha! "Then why you always actin' so stank whenever I try and talk to you?" Jeezus crackers! Is it baby a ninja week and no one told me. "Fine Jermaine, jump out and let's chat." I swear if he made me regret it, I'd chop him in tha throat, knee dem balls and mace his ass. Jermaine hopped out, smile wide and bopped up on tha sidewalk. "A'ight, talk." I spat, foot tappin'. "Whas sup?" Whas sup? Is he serious right now? "Nothin', chillin'." "So, where you headin'? Whatchu 'bout to get into?" Whoa, just cause you wordin' shit different don't mean I'ma answer different, stupid ass. "Didn't I just tell yo ass I ain't doin' shit, I'm chillin'. What I need to do, speak dick in my ass language?" That's right, I took it there, and what! Jermaine frowned. "Fuck outta here with that gay shit, a nigga tryina see whats up with me and you." I almost choked on my damn tongue. Laughin', I stared at his dick in tha booty self, damn near in tears. "Fuck so funny Taylor?" "You nigga. Yo ass must've forgot I saw you comin' from Donell's. Tha whole hood knows Donell's gay.." "Dat nigga owed me money for some clothes my crew boosted." He quickly inserted. Just come out and admit yo ass gay ninja. If you like slobbin' on dick and gobblin' balls more than me, yo behind is gay boo. Plus, nobody ever sees you wit' females unless yo boostin' hoes on ya'll way to steal some shit. "Ah unh. Well anyway, I'm good; a bitch got enough dudes on the rotate list, but I'll keep in mind that you're interested a'ight." Turnin' to walk away, I'm halted by Jermaine snatchin' my arm. The switch jiggled. See. This why you can't be nice to niggas, you give 'em any play and they oversteppin' boundaries and shit. I snatched my arm away, wincin' a lil. "Back up nucca, did I give permission to touch me? No. Now I tried to be nice, Lord knows I did, but you wanna take it there, so God damn it, let's take it there!" I blasted, switch all the way up and stuck in position. "And just for tha record, I'd never fuck yo ass, yo ass a pretender boo and Taylor don't do those, okay. You pretend you're hard body, out here makin' big moves; only thing big on you is tha shit fallin' in tha toilet. You pretend you'll fight and shoot anyone who disrespects, well Donell did and I ain't seen you set him skraight yet boo, why? Cause yo ass still tiptoeing through to hide the salaami. You pretend you're from the streets, when errbody knows yo ass from New Hampshire and yo family got dough. You pretend you're all dat but you not boo, so step tha fuck off!" Face heated, Jermaine's jaw twisted back and forth. "Fuck you Taylor, nobody wants yo old ass. You ain't wifey material, all you can pull is youngins, cause dey don't know no better!" He barked like it was suppose to make me cower in fear. Not! "Don't be J boo, 'cause I can get any Johnson I put these eyes on. So I'ma let you marinate on this for a moment." I sprayed his ass smack in eyes, nose and mouth when he opened it to yell in pain; added a kick to tha balls and before Jermaine hit tha ground, a chop to tha throat. Never let it be said I ain't a woman of my word. *

CHAPTER 15

'Damn..' thought Dove, 'I can get used to this shit right here.'. Layin' in Hex's bed, Dove wasn't even sure how she'd wound up at his place. Last thing she remembered was sitting on a custies lap, him telling her he was from Philly, had heard how Connecticut bitches put it down and offered her nine hundred to sample. A hazy thought flashed of Hex in the parking lot, having words with Philly before taking her by the hand and leading her towards his Escalade. Spreading her thighs, Dove patted her pride and joy, stuck one finger inside and felt no soreness. Withdrawing finger showed only her juices, so she ascertained no sex had transpired lastnight. Maybe she'd been too high to get some and Hex wanted to wait until she was sober. The thought caused a smile and delicious pang between her thighs. The door opened and in walked Hex, carrying a tray laden with something that set her tummy to growling. "Good, you're woke." greeted Hex, sitting tray atop her legs. "Mornin', how'd I get here and where is here?" asked Dove while eyin' scrambled eggs that looked kinda dry, toast a smidgen away from bein' burnt and a few slices of turkey bacon. "I didn't know if you drank coffee and tea, so I just brought you a glass of apple juice and here, is my place, I brought you here lastnight, dat nigga you was wit' dropped a roofie in yo drink. He and his three pals planned on havin' a good time, starrin' you." Dove's eyes widened in joy and surprise. Joy cause niggas really wanted a taste and would go through extreme lengths; take that Taylor! And surprise, 'cause Hex cared enough to rescue her. That got pussy juices flowin'. "Thanks Hex. guess I need to be more careful." Truthfully Dove knew about the roofie, she hadn't known about the three other penises though. "So now what?" Inquired Dove, then bit into a piece of bacon, almost gaggin' from its leathery flavor. Grabbin' apple juice Dove chugged down half tha glass then burped. "Is it okay if I take a shower?" Sayin' anythin' to get away from that horrible ass breakfast Hex had made. "Yeah, it's through there." he pointed at an ajoined door half open. "I've got some sweats and a tee shirt you can wear." "Thanks." Dove slid out of bed in a panty and bra set, but didn't bother to ask if she or he had removed her clothing. Hex's bathroom was plenty damn basic, pictureless plain white walls, no matching towels or rugs. Dove opened the cabinet beneath the sink and saw nothing but a six pack roll of tissue, a can of Ajax and a toilet brush. Turning on the shower, she hurriedly opened medicine cabinet and only saw a new toothbrush, tube of Colgate and a bottle of Excedrin. Strippin' from her bra and panties, Dove grabbed a wash cloth and gave it a sniff. It smelled clean, so she scooped up Dove soap and stepped inside. The door opened releasing steam. "Hey." Dove poked her head out tha shower curtain. "Here's the clothes." Dove's eyes drank Hex in. "Care to join me?" she huskily asked and felt her eyes widen when Hex stepped fully inside, closed the door and yanked wifebeater over his head; revealing a taut six pack, firm chest and corded muscular arms. When he shucked basketball shorts and boxers, Dove felt her throat seize. Nine and a half veiny inches hung between muscled thighs. Hex yanked open the curtain, stepped inside, then slid it closed. One hand reached out, yanked her so close soapy breasts smooshed against hair free chest. "This whatchu want?" He asked, eyes unreadable. "Hell yeah I want it all and then some. Can you handle that?" Hex spun her around until her face met water, kicked her legs apart and ordered, "Bend over." Dove reached for ankles, then swallowed a scream of pleasure pain as all that meat plowed in to the hilt stretching and filling her completely. "Sss." hissed Dove as Hex grabbed her hips and started grinding. "Umm, that feels so good." ended with a yelp. Hex switched up and started deep stroking, hitting every corner with hard shaft. Her eyes popped open when her feet left the shower floor. "Hold them legs open." he ordered, then started hitting it slow, then fast, mixed in a lil grinding and had Dove coming back to back from Hex banging the hell outta her g-spot. "Uh, sss, yess." Dove cried, tryin' to keep up and show Hex she wasn't an amateur and failing miserably. "Shit!" Before Dove knew it, Hex had turned her facing him, threw her legs up so they rested against his torso and kept stroking. Digging deep, lips latched onto her nipple, teasing with tongue before teeth gently nibbled, making her insides curl tightly in a knot of pleasure. Mouth wide, eyes rolling, Dove swore she heard bells and whistles as her body neared orgasm. "Fuck!" Hex roared, sac tightening. The water turned cold long ago, but neither noticed as they raced towards the finish line. Faster, deeper, grinding, slow thrusts on and on until an earth shaking release weakened knees and Hex sunk to the shower floor. * Hex spent the whole day with Dove. They ordered The Perfect Guy on cable, had sex, played strip poker, had sex. Dove whipped up homemade mash potatoes and meatloaf, while Hex sexed her and demanded, "Don't burn shit." while doin' it. By the time he dropped Dove back at the club to get her car she was walkin' wide legged and beyond sated. * "Hey stranger, you don't know nobody no more?" Asked Glenda, who stood on the other side of the door, hands on hips. Groggy, Dove blinked, tryin a get her brain to compute. A yawn slid out. "Hunh? What time is it?" Glenda stepped inside. "It's nine pm. Why you still in bed, you sick? Wait, you got company don't you, ole nasty butt." joked Glenda then leaned and sniffed Dove's neck. "Eww, tha hell you doin'?" snapped Dove. "Calm down jeez, I'm just playin'. Anyway, wanna hit tha club tonight? Its Thursday, you're off work right?" "Uh yeah, where and is you know who rollin'?" asked Dove, voice full of attitude. Glenda flopped on Dove's couch. "Girl whats yo beef wit' Tay'? I mean seriously, tha girls done nothin' to you for you to be carryin' so much attitude." Stressed Glenda. Dove smacked her lips, strolled to the couch, took a seat and yanked a freshly lit cigarette from Glenda's lips. "Yoink, thanks, I need it more then you especially if its discuss Taylor hour." "See, all tart n dry.." "She's fake okay. Taylor's fake, she's not a true friend and anyone who believes different will find out the hard way in the end." snapped Dove. Glenda lit another cigarette. "Ok, well what'd she do to turn you into who you've become?" "Fuck you mean? I haven't changed, she did; always braggin' 'bout her dudes and what they got her. 'Ooo did ya'll see my two engagement rings or ooo ya'll wanna ride in my car', please." she snorted. "Taylor's just an old slore who needs to sit it down and try and be a mother to Kione instead of dick chasin'." Cigarette finished, Glenda stood and started for the door. "Girl I can't wit' you okay. To answer yo question, yeah she'll probably come we always go together; three the hard way, three muskateers. Wear somethin' cute. I'll ride with Tay' since we live next door to each other, so meet us there." The door closed behind her. * Club 21 was the happs on a Thursday night. It was twenty-one and up so it was always crowded; and after a few drinks and any lil thing could and would set shit off, which usually spread outside, escalating until the law arrived to disperse theruckus with pepper spray and police dogs. Inside was damn near standing room only with jewelry blinging at every turn, drinks flowed, daps and hugs were given, while groups of females trotted off to the restroom to gossip and get freaky in the stall. The price to enter tonight was fifteen big ones and nobody had a problem paying it to come inside and pick their entertainment once the club closed. Dove arrived, lookin' good after a quick visit to Chen's which had soured her mood because he kept askin' where was his home skillet Taylor. She wore a lemon yellow bandage dress she'd had altered so that the hemline rested right beneath ass cheeks and lemon wedge heels, her hair done in spiral curls. Glenda suddenly appeared, colored drink already half gone in hand. The two air kissed. "Hey now Dove. I'm lovin' that dress girlie, work it!" shouted Glenda who wore chocolate riding pants, black and chocolate riding boots and a black sheer shirt with two chocolate pockets covering her breasts; her hair in block braids and held back with chocolate headband.

'Ump,' thought Dove. 'Glenda finally upgraded, 'bout damn time.' "You look really nice." Glenda beamed, "Thanks. C'mon lets head to tha bar, I need a refill." Dove fell in step, wonderin' where Taylor's triflin' ass was at; probably busy on her knees somewhere. Glenda got a glass of Remy with a splash of Coke, while Dove had a Hennessey on ice. Turning, Dove felt her jaw drop and anger surge through her insides. "Dis bitch," she uttered, not carin' who fuckin' heard. Taylor wore the I Dream Of Jeannie ensemble, complete with ponytail! Her eyes zeroed in searchin' for any flaw no matter how small. Light pink harem pants that in light showed its sheerness and a pink sheer bra with a dark pink short jacket. The old bat even wore flats like Jeannie. If hate could fly across the club and kill Taylor, Dove's night would be perfect. "Wow! Tay' looks amazin'!" Glenda yelled over Ariana Grande, her words causin' Dove's temples to throb. I peeped Dove's ole hatin' ass, along wit a bunch a hoes who wished they could wear somethin' like this and look as good as moi. But chu can't boo, cause don't nobody wanna see stretch marked boobs that barely sit up, cause they're saggy as hell, or a belly that hadn't been flat since birth. Knife wounds, razor scars, bullet marks, yo shit lookin' like a traffic jam on I-94. Don't embarrass yoself hunny, I'm just sayin'. Walkin' up, smile bright, I gave Glenda a hug, Dove a nod and walked towards crowded bar for the first drank of many. Some semi cutie bumped me and then gone over talk me like I ain't orderin', poof nucca, be gone fo' tha Jeannie in me hurts yo feelins'. "Yo!" Dude yelled, "let me get some bottle action, these cump buyin' mofos can wait!" He barked, like he was Lebron or some damn body. "Xcuse you, but she was takin' my order," I snapped cause he kinda cute don't mean he can go up befo' greatness, I'm just sayin'. Funny colored eyes that must've been contacts 'cause I ain't neva seen dem shits on a black man dragged up and down my frame before a smirk appeared. "Shouldn't yo old ass be in a club more yo speed, they don't play James Brown up in here grandma." Then turned back to the bartender and ordered Cristal, Ace of Spades and that 1738 dead eye be singin' 'bout. Ooo I know dis Lurch lookin' ninja ain't tryina do me! "Listen here Lurch, just 'cause you got a lil cake and you out celebratin' yo release from the zoo, don't mean come fo' me. You don't know me boo and I fo' damn sure don't wanna know yo over grown foreheaded ass. Yeah I'm old, anddd? Don't hate 'cause I look betta than all tha beasts in yo party, especially the red lip batfish you wit' cause that's all you'll ever pull; unless there's a bag over yo head and a bunch a cash involved." Pow! Fists balled, dude started breathin' all hard, like he was 'bout to turn into tha Incredible Hulk. Chile please, yo ass wanna jump, jump. Stop wastin' time swellin' up 'cause tha bigger they are, tha harder they fall and his ass gone crash to tha floor when I crack his ass wit' one of them bottles he coppin'.

Another slender dude rushed up, guess he saw our confrontation. That's right save him boo, from bein' hella embarrassed and clowned cause Taylor plays no games wit' tha dis-respect-ful. "Yo Wayne, chill yo! C'mon back to our table I'll get our drinks." he pleaded, eyes beggin' dude to listen to him. "Eight fifty." said the waitress after tappin' my shoulder. "Hold on hunny, let me take care of this right quick." Rule one while in the club: Never turn yo back on a mafucka 'cause they'll stab you in it. "Yeah, a'ight handle that 'cause I beat old bitches too." He spat, gave me another look and disappeared in the crowd. "Sorry 'bout that. Wayne's had a fucked up night, he was just suspended from Charlie Jeez's detail. Let me buy you a drink." Dude rushed out. Charlie Jeez was some lil Jamaican nigglet who was from Hartford, he'd scored big last summer wit' three hit singles. Whoopty fuckin' do. Just get my drank and get out my face, okay. Anyhoo, drank in hand, I strolled around finally locatin' Dove and Glenda over by the dancefloor. I started to blast both of 'em for bouncin' on me, then chucked it up, filed it away and was ready to get my party on. "Everythin' a'ight?" asked Dove, hope glistenin' that I'd been beat down in her eyes. No suck luck sweetie, I'm still standin' boo and lookin' damn good while doin' it. "I'm good." Short and sweet; and her ass betta be glad she ain't get dis glass to tha face. That scrawny kid, July or August started playin' and Dove and Glenda hit tha floor; I couldn't stand his music or his face for that matter. Somethin' 'bout dem bag of bones made my skin crawl hunny; so I turned down a bunch of dance requests 'cause September don't deserve havin' all this on tha dancefloor. Decidin' to continue strollin', I took in tha barely dressed, tha shoulda left that outfit in tha closet; tha drunk and actin' a fool and more. Ump, just tasteless boo. Have some shame cause a half shirt and leggins' on two hundred and forty pounds ain't a good look when yo belly hangin' over yo snacks. I'm just sayin'. Now I'm over by VIP and November's still goin', when tha hairs on my arm stand up and holla. Glancin' round tha packed VIP, I catch Lurch glarin' at me while yellin' somethin' to a chick who in turn glared my way and then started flappin'. I ain't hear shit cause 21 was loud as fuck, nor was I worried 'bout it. I knew Dove's ass was mia if jumpin' popped off and most likely she'd make sure Glenda's back was turned or somethin'. It's okay though, I'll take an L; but best believe every time I saw 'em I'm runnin' up. B. Smythe's 'Creep' came on so I hit tha dancefloor over by tha mirrors to keep an eye on my back by my damn self. Cause tha only thang I'm scared of is grey pussy hairs and Mizani not havin' my hair color. I'm just sayin'. The music switched and my favorite music loudly boomed. Reggae, I loved tha bass. I couldn't understand much of what was bein' said, but what I do know is this, reggae music artists today are wack. All soft voiced, singin' love songs and shit while yesteryears got chu up on yo feet or had you dancin' in yo seat. I do like Gage though, his song 'Throat' is my anthem. I'm groovin', sippin' on a wine cooler when I see two ragamuffins approachin', mean mugs in place. One reached out to grab swayin' ponytail and I quickly turned; 'cause I don't play dem catfight hair pullin' games. "Yo bitch, you got a problem wit' my man Wayne?!" One loudly spat. "Girl bye, ain't nobody studyin' yo ugly, rude ass Guila Monster." the other chicks nostril flared at the insult. Ooo chile, don't do that. Yo joint looks like you'll suck all tha oxygen from tha room. I'm just sayin'. "Fuck you here for grandma, ain't it past yo curfew?" I ain't wit' tha back and forth, fuck it, I swung my wine cooler, catchin' her dead between them big ass eyes she got. Someone yelled as chick two ran up throwin' some heavy ass blows. We was goin' toe to toe, when bottle to tha face staggered to her feet, wobbled and charged like a ragin' bull. Seein' her comin', I moved two steps to tha left just in time and her ass went head first right into tha mirror. Chick two swung, shakin' shit up wit' a blow to my chin. I bit my tongue hard as hell. Pissed, I punched her in the gibblets forcin' out rank breath and a slew of liquor that splashed on my outfit. Even madder, cause China's girl charged my ass one hundred and fifty bucks to make it, was now ruined; so I grabbed that big bitches weave and ran her ass into another mirror, tha shit shattered. Chick one was up, forehead bleedin' and ready for payback. Shit, my ass gettin' tired, where tha hells security?! Chick one punched me in tha side so hard I spun around and caught a blow to tha jaw. Aww shit, I'm in trouble. Suddenly chick two was bein' pummeled wit' a chair bein' swung by Glenda. Yes! I planned on doin' somethin' nice fo' my girl. Fuck Dove's fake ass! Security finally arrived, givin' me a chance to catch my breath and regroup. Security escorted me and Glenda out first; talkin' 'bout 'we're banned unless we paid half of the damages'. Hunny please, ya'll can keep this kiddy club, cause I ain't givin' up none of these coins okay. Outside we farted around til' I saw them hoes come outside, poppin' shit and bleedin', they walked over to a green Dodge Charger; sat for a sec, revved tha engine then yerked off wit' a squeal of tires. *

CHAPTER 16

Once again Taylor's ass walked away without serious injury, stewed Dove as she lay in Hex's bed. She couldn't even enjoy pullin' his sexy ballin' ass because Taylor constantly popped in her thoughts. Even Glenda was team Taylor. She'd had tha nerve to feel some type because she'd wanted no parts of helpin' Taylor; choosin' instead to go smoke a cigarette outside. "Fuck both them bitches." muttered Dove while grillin' tha ceilin' for answers. Hex had asked her to stop by, only for him to leave five minutes later citing, 'business before pleasure.'; so fuckin' his brains out was a no go at least for now. Decidin' to snoop around, Dove hopped out of bed and since already in tha bedroom, she started there. Word was Hex owned properties all over, so chances were there might not even be anythin' of worth here to pilfer. Butt jigglin', Dove opened a chest of drawers and began searchin' beneath boxers, socks, tees and wifebeaters and so far, bumpkus. Leavin' tha dresser, Dove stomped over to Hex's closet; already frustrated and ready to yank her hair out. His closet was huge and filled wit' color coordinated shirts, jeans and a revolvin' shoe rack that held sneakers, loafers and dress shoes. Grabbin' a foot stool, Dove started on tha shelf which held hats and shoe boxes, tha first two boxes yielded nothin' but a bunch of papers and old newspaper clippins' she had no interest in readin'. But box five had a big grin formin'; Money, neatly banded by a thick rubberbands. Snatchin' a stack Dove quickly thumbed through it, one thousand, there were twenty stacks inside the box. Should she? 'Nah Dove, don't be greedy.' she told herself, then took only one just in case Hex needed to go in tha box for some odd reason. *

Fuckin' ugly hoes got my chin, jaw and forehead three different colors. Why ugly chicks always wanna damage a pretty girl's face? Hell, they'll still be ugly tha next day and the day after while us cute ones heal up and are good as new. Tha shit makes no damn sense if you ask me. I'm just sayin'. Them hoes betta thank the ugly Gods I ain't rockin' black eyes and shit, cause I'd be forced to take out my granny's .45 named Betsey. Any damn way, it had been five days since tha fight and today was Glenda's birthday. No one knew I still had armored truck robbery money left; not much after hirin' Mason a top notch lawyer and what not. I rarely touched it, cause niggas I fucked wit' paid lovely; so I was sittin' on $50,000 which I refused to use towards ass injections. Speakin' of, I only needed ten big ones and it was on! So my plan today was to treat Glenda for tha whole dang day; breakfast, Chen's, lunch, shoppin', hair salon, dinner and finally tha club. * Nine am and music blared from Glenda's, today she was thirty, grown up status. Today was all about her, but tomorrow she'd sit Marcus down and ask him if his future included her. She needed to know before sharing tha pregnancy test taken two hours ago. Just the thought plastered a dreamy smile on her face. Here was her chance, another baby to love her, to be spoiled. She wouldn't mess up this time by leaving her child with any and everyone in order to hang in the streets and party. Taking a seat on the couch, Glenda debated on what to do today besides getting turned up of course. Marcus had gotten a job working for the city's santitation department and couldn't get the day off. A knock sounded at her kitchen door. Glenda danced the whole way there to Mary J's 'Whats The 411' album. Lifting the curtain, her lips twisted. Okra. Fuck her miserable ass wanted? Everytime Marcus stepped outside, her fat ass would pop up, begging Marcus to tell her why they broke up; why she couldn't have another chance? Blah, blah, blah. Her ass seemed to forget she had Marcus first. Taking a calming breath, Glenda opened the door. "Can I help you?" Okra eyed her up and down, no doubt seeing something she'd never be, thin. "Is Marcus here?" 'Tha nerve of this girl.' thought Glenda. "No, he isn't, is there something I can help you wit'?" Okra muttered something she couldn't hear, then snapped out. "I doubt it. Don't you think you've done enough already?" "Excuse me?" Glenda said, not sure if she'd heard right. "Bitch you heard me, you man stealin' tramp." Jaw dropped in astonishment, here it was her birthday and trouble comes knocking before the day started good. Anger bubbled to the surface. "Okra, I advise you to get tha hell away from my door wit' this bullshit. I ain't in tha mood." "Girl bye, who gives a shit what chu in tha mood for. I came to see Marcus, to speak wit' Marcus, to give Marcus his mail, not to listen to you cryin' 'bout cho damn mood. Take a Xanax and go lay tha fuck down!" yelled Okra, big breasts heavin'. Trying to swallow her anger, Glenda tried again. "Listen Okra, I'm busy and don't have time for yo jealous rantin' and ravin'. Now either hand over tha mail or beat it." "Beat it.....I'd love to." said Okra and punched Glenda so hard in the chest she flew back into her kitchen, slid into the stove where she smacked the back of her head on the oven's handle. Scramblin' to her feet, head throbbin', Glenda grabbed her baby mallet used to tenderize meat and charged wit' a banshee type yell. The hoods silent alarm that there was a fight in progress had mafuckas scramblin' for a front row seat. Glenda clunked Okra atop the head, once, twice, three times before her thick melon sprang a leak. "I'm tired of bitches like you assumin' cause I get a check

I'm a punk. Well yo ass whoopin' gonna be a lesson to all, don't fuck wit' Glenda!" She roared, dropped the mallet and took it to Okra's face and stomach with gut wrenchin' stomps. I was comin' from in back of tha Courts wit' a couple a bags of weed for me and Glenda when I spot her through tha crowd beatin' fire outta Okra's ass. Runnin' before she really did some damage and spent her birthday behind bars. I pushed my way through, grabbed Glenda, almost trippin' over a mallet in tha process; so I scooped it up and pulled Glenda over to my place while she cursed and threatened Okra as the watchers grumbled and dispersed. * An hour later, bag and a half in our system, Glenda and I headed over to Ihop (her choice) for breakfast. Once there we ordered, then I had to sit and listen, again while Glenda told me what happened. Thank the food gawds our shit arrived cause how many ways can you tell tha same story? I'm just sayin'. Ooo, I'm 'bout to tear these pancakes, sausage and hash browns downn! Pickin' up a fork, I glance up and who do I see weavin' through tables headed in our direction? Dove. I swear tha bitch a stalker. "Don't be mad." Glenda quickly said. "I invited her. Please be nice Tay', it's my birthday." Puppy dog look and flutter of lashes had me crackin' up. "Okay, but only cause it's your day." "Hey ya'll." Dove greeted, then slid into tha booth beside Glenda. That's right boo, yo ass know betta than to sit over here 'cause I'll bite cho fuckin' face off. Fuck wit' me if you want.

"Hey." "Thanks for comin' Dove. Are you gonna hang out wit' us all day?" Glenda asked; my ears perked up. Dats a good got damn question. "Maybe, what ya'll doin'?" Glenda looked at me, deep sigh. "Breakfast, Chen's.." "Girll you're gonna love that shit! Tay' took me there once and every chance I get I go back. I can't afford tha works, but a Mani, Pedi and I'm good." Toe jam on a cracker! Could she shut tha fuck up! I swore it was Glenda's b-day, not listen to this chick spill what she'd had done at Chen's. Who cared she had dem eagle claws filed down. Niggas everywhere grateful cause she was leavin' hella scars boo, I'm just sayin'. "Eh hem." I cleared my throat. "After Chen's we'll do lunch. After lunch a lil shoppin', then to the hair salon; then dinner and then we'll hit tha club." Dove knew Tay' was tryina be funny cause she thought she was broke. Ha! 'Jokes on you' thought Dove 'cause she had a lil somethin' in her pocket. Plus, if treatin' were involved, there were a cute pair of nine hundred dollar heels Glenda wanted and Dove Mitchell would be tha one to buy 'em. * True to my word, we hit up every spot I mentioned and when we were done, Glenda looked and felt like a new woman. Hell, b-day or not, Marcus might not let her ass outside tonight. I'm just saying.............................

CHAPTER 17

Dove walked around the property, heels snagging on weeds as she walked. The Golden Years retirement home had been closed for years. Its eighteen rooms, kitchen, office and two acres was more than enough. "And you're willing to fix it up to suit my needs?" Dove asked the shifty eyed owner again. "Sure, sure, whatever you need, as long as the main structure stays the same." Noticing a rat scampering across the floor, Dove hesitated as if changing her mind. Seeing it, the owner Bob Greene quickly said, "The place has been closed since the 80's. Theres no doubt a lotta four, six and eight legged creatures running round, but I'll take care of it, no charge." Greed shone from green eyes in anticipation of making the sale. His wife Connie, God bless her, but good riddance, had passed in '77 leaving him Golden Years, which he'd promptly set about closing after kicking out its tenants. "Okay, deal, but I want everything in writing, that we just discussed and a date on when your part will be complete." "You have yourself a deal." * Feeling good now that her plan was in effect, Dove stopped at T-Boe's bar and grill for a lil afternoon drink. Parking on Baltimore Street and the Ave, Dove stuck a stiletto on the pavement, walked up to T-Boe's doors and stepped inside to the sounds of Junior Walker and the All-Stars. Old fogies lined the bar, no doubt remembering the '50's. Her nose wrinkled from the scents of Ben Gay and cologne, yuck! "Can I help you pretty lady?" asked a salty haired codger, the whites of his eyes a dull brown. Containing a shiver as these could be potential clients, if Viagra worked in there favor, she smiled. "Uh..let me get a Sex On The Beach." a dozen wrinkles appeared across his forehead. "Sex on the beach? Oh no, we don't sell those kinds of drinks." Astounded, Dove stared back, 'those kinds, fuck he means, it's a real fuckin' drink'. She thought. "Well we have beer of course, Cognac, Brandy, Rum, Vodka, things like that." Feeling her good mood spoiling, Dove quickly ordered a Vodka and orange juice. The door opened and in walked Kione. "You're late," he snapped, "I've been here forty-five minutes and was just about to leave when I saw your car." "Shut up and sit down." Kione glared, looking like he warred with himself on knocking her on her ass before finally taking a seat at the bar. "A'ight, I'm here, fuck you want?" Kione's testiness was startin' to piss her off.

"Fuck is yo problem Kione?" He smirked. "You. You're my problem, you're just like my mother." he threw up quotation marks. "Y'all out for self and don't give two fucks about me." 'True. Were his lil feelings hurt? Grow up nigglet; lifes hard, then you die.' Thought Dove. "Sorry you feel that way, I've just been busy, I wasn't purposely ignorin' you. Besides, if I wasn't thinkin' 'bout you, you wouldn't be here right now." lied Dove. Kione was there because he was easy to manipulate, he was desperate for a mommy figure and to be closer to Taylor or any of her friends. Who was she to deny him? * August fifth rolled around and I was ready to party for tha next twenty-six days. Why? I ain't need a reason boo, its what I do. Syke, its my d.o.b.; the day all nuccas realized greatness had arrived, oh, you ain't know. I'm a great dresser, my walk alone is so great I gotta beat 'em off wit' a get back stick; my mouth games great cause a nucca'll tap out soon as I latch on and don't get me started on what da pus' do okay. Friday I'd be flyin' out to Atlanta. That's right a bitch reached her goal and was ready to get dese cakes baked, frosted and ready to clap on a nuccas face! Ha! After doin' my homework I decided to go wit' that doctor from Lifetimes 'Atlanta Plastic.' Babyy Dr. Marcus Crawford can get it okay. Ump, damn sexy, chocolate bastard got my pussy hummin'. Y'all all ready knows I like 'em chocolate huntie, ump! Sperm tastes like Hershey's meltin' on my tongue. Yess lawd, let

143

Dr. Crawford lay hands on dese cakes, and feel free to test drive 'em too boo. Amen. I'd done a lil snoopin' and found out he was married, which wasn't my problem; had two kids, again, not my problem, 'cause I just wanted to borrow him for a few hours, then I'd send him home to shoot hoops wit' junior. He's also six years past my cut off, but I'll make an exception for him. Hell, I won't even hit up them fat ass pockets! I'm just sayin'. Hol' on I gotta go change my drawers, Dr. Crawford done got me all worked tha hell up... * "Happy birthday!" Glenda yelled. She sat an ice cream cake on tha table and I burst out laughin' at tha sight of a big, long, ding dong drippin' cum atop it. "Girl no you didn't! I know whoever took your order was hella horny!" Glenda laughed. "Actually it was a guy named Amos who said his boyfriends dick was bigger." she said wit' straight face before crackin' up. A minute later, Rosalie was knockin' I let her ass in, but told her tha minute she got it f'd up it was a wrap. Her usual beggin' ass surprised me when she pulled out four dime bags, and not no reg, but some shit so good half an L had me right gotdamn it! * The Courts threw me an impromptu party; pullin' food from deep freezers, whippin' up salads and makin' liquor runs, and I tried to drink a lil of everythin' on tha table xcept fo' that nasty ass peach flavored Paulie. Ugh! Shit tasted like three cups of sour, tart ass sperm; it ain't taste nothin' like fuckin' peaches. Hell, my ass crack tasted more like peaches than that bullshit. I'm just sayin'. Anyhoo, a coupla haters were in attendance, like Toni and Kelly, Brenda, Barbara, Sonya and Tiffani. Baby I could go all day 'bout these hatin' hoes who ain't got enough courage to say what they feel; scary bitches I swear. A tall, muscled piece of man meat walked up. "Sup Tay', happy b-day." Chocolate. No wonder Brenda was lookin' all kinds of crazy. Wonder what kinda tricks she did to get his ass back. "Chillin' nigga, you got somethin' fo' me, or you just gone stand there droolin'?" Chocolate smiled. "Yeah I got somethin' for you alright, if you can handle it." Ooo no boo, I know your jack rabbit ass ain't frontin' like you slangin' King Kong dick. Don't do it boo, 'cause you don't want me to tell how you was shakin', shiverin', cryin' and ballin' up like a fetus okay. "Really?" sip of Corona. "You done got cho skills up hunh?" Chocolate grabbed his penis and gave a squeeze, tryina make it look bigga than it was. Please, it's an illusion, a mirage; okay. Shit, I still ain't figured out why they call his ass Chocolate when he's a brown skinned mafucka. Brenda's ole horse faced ass walked up lookin' like Mr. Ed. "Hey Taylor." she said all dry, like it was supposed to hurt my feelins'. She obviously ain't heard 'bout me, I hurt feelins', not the other way around. This chile wasn't worth a response, so I tuned Brenda's ass out, finished my Corona and made my way inside to hit tha bathroom. Ump, let me tell ya, takin' a pee when drinkin' is one of tha best feelins'! Wipin', I flushed, stood and pulled up thong and down skirt; washed my hands, opened tha door and swung. "Oomp." "Fuck you doin' in my shit Chocolate!" Rubbin' cheek, his ass backed me up til' he was fully inside, then kicked tha door shut. "Bend over, let me hit it right quick." Smirk, he's right 'bout that. "Nah playa, ain't Brenda outside." "So." Was this ninja serious? A'ight let me see what he's workin' wit'. So I did as requested and bent over, hands atop commode. Chocolate moaned, yanked down b-ball shorts, boxers and out sprang a kids toy; six pencil thin inches he made jump like that was gonna impress me, snort. You wanna impress me, last longer than your dick length boo, okay. 'Cause that right there ain't even a snack boo, its like openin' a can of Vienna's and seein' only one inside. I'm just sayin'. It took dis ninja a hot second to roll on a condom and four tugs to rip off my thong. That's the Bat Signal right there that ain't shit changed, getcho weight up boo. "Need some help?" Damn right I asked. Damn pussy juices dryin' up waitin' on his slow ass. Nigga so slow he came in third in a two-man race. He so slow I thought his ass was movin' backwards. I finally feel him slide tha head in wit' a grunt, next thing I know his ass starts howlin' and shit. Wait....what? Did I blink? Shit, maybe I'm still outside and tha weed I smoked got me trippin'. Like how tha hell you beat yo own record nigga? That had to be tha fastest cum in tha world, somebody call Guinness Book of World Records. Tsk, and yo ass got tha nerve to rip off my thong like we 'bout to get shit poppin'. I look over my shoulder and Chocolate's breathin' all hard when a loud knock sounded at my bathroom door. Chocolate went to yank off condom and tha door swung open smackin' him in tha shoulder. "Nah! This ain't goin' down again bitch!" screamed Brenda, damn near foamin' at tha mouth. "I turn my back for one second and yo white livered old ass up here on my mans dick!" Chocolate hurriedly pulled up clothin', "its not what you think bae.." "Stupid. You're still wearin' tha condom, so what else can it be?!" she screamed so loud I know them vocals were hurtin'. "I..we..she was.." Brenda gave a war cry and started swingin', catchin' Chocolate all upside tha side of his face, then changed it up and swung on me. Uh, wrong boo, not today. Blockin' that ameteur punch, I showed Brenda's ass how its done. Aware of Chocolate scramblin' from tha bathroom, down tha stairs and out tha door while I beat his girls face in; then grabbed a handful of hair and drug her ass down tha stairs, through tha kitchen and out tha door. Leavin' her where she lay, resumed my seat and continued partyin'. *

CHAPTER 18

Dancing for Hex had paid so good there was no need to continue stealing from Hex's shoe box. In fact, feeling guilty, Dove started putting the money she'd borrowed back; well, almost until Hex went in the box, realized money was unaccounted for and stomped down to his basement and pulled up security footage of inside and out. By the time he saw what he needed to see, his temples throbbed while his hands itched to wrap around her fuckin' throat. Hours later he was still stewing as he watched Taylor talk and flirt wit big spenders up in VIP. Dove had been scheduled, but so far she was a no call no show, which pissed him off anew. "Yo Hex, man I'm lovin' dis skrip club." yelled Hex's second in command, Larry Love. Most people slept on Larry as he barely cleared the five-foot mark, was slimly built and soft spoken; unless buzzing on weed and or booze and pills. "Glad you like it." Larry Love took a seat. "Mann, when you gone hook yo boy up?!" Hex gave a small smile. "I got you. Who you want, caramel, toffee.." "Nah, nah," he cut in. "hook me up wit' that sexy bitch Tay'. Man I heard she's a super freak!" Hex chuckled. "I don't know 'bout that, you'd have better luck trying on your own." "Okay, okay, just throwin' out I might need a lil help." said Larry Love, big smile on his face. Taylor walked up. "Can I get cha anythin' to drink?" Hex cleared his throat, urgin' his boy to go for it. "A Bud and yo digits." Damn that was lame. I eyed his short, mixed mutt ass. Larry was half black and half Hispanic. He kept his curly, jet black, curly locks in a ponytail that rested between shoulder blades, round grey eyes and full lips on a hairless face. "How old are you?" Larry Love stared, stumped by my question, which was pissin' me off. Do I need to break out some sign language, pull Braille out my cootch, what! "Sorry, I'm twenty six." Hmm, a year over. "What size shoe you wear?" I asked, fuckin' wit' him cause that hand, feet shit was a fairy tale, trust. "Nine, why? what that got to do with me diggin' yo guts out." My eyes widened and tha kitty sat to attention. Alright now boo, talk that good shit. My snacks started singin' 'you got me feenin, feenin' to ride that dick, fee-innn to slob on yo balls...damn what he say? Oh yeah, size nine, gut digger, got it. "860-997-xxxx call me boo, I'll be right back wit' yo beer." Hex smiled, happy for his boy. "Good lookin'. Yo, mann I'ma tear her shit talkin' ass out tha frame!" Minutes later beer in hand, I strutted cross tha floor just as one of them hoes crossed my path. So wit' no hesitation I reached out and touched that hoe. Beer splashed all over her hair and blouse, followed by glass when I clunked her ass again, followed by a punch. "Oh you must've fo'got I owe you and yo ugly partner an ass whoopin'! Ya'll like jumpin' bitches right? Well watch me work, cause I don't need no one to help me beat dat ass!" I roared, peltin' her ass left and right wit' fists and glasses and bottles patrons had sittin' atop tables. People were jumpin' out tha way as I beat her ass from over by tha dancefloor, all the way damn near to VIP; only stoppin' when this swole ass bouncer named Archie yanked me off her ole lumped up ass. Hex approached lookin' all irate n shit. "My office, now!" He barked wit' Larry Love bringin' up tha rear. "Fuck is wrong wit' you Taylor! You in here tearin' my shit up. I hired you to be classy, if I wanted ghetto I would've hired Dove's ass." he snapped. Well excuse tha hell outta me, but what real woman would've let ole gurl walk past and not do nothin'? None! "That cow and her friend jumped me a few months back. I saw her ole beefy ass and jumped dead on dat ass and I'd do it again. So fire me, cause I don't give a flyin' fuck nucca!" I blasted back. Hex don't scare me, he might have his yes man under control, but I ain't tha one. "I'm not gonna fire you Tay'. Just go home, take a few days off and get cho mind right." You ain't gotta tell me twice, peace, I'm out! * "Damn nigga. It's been what, a year since I told yo crazy ass to lose my number and here you are, callin' again? Fuck you need a house to fall on yo ass or sumthin'?" Brandon's ole stalkin' ass. I should've known the silence was too good to be true. "Hurry up Tay', damn." griped Glenda. She and I were teamed up against Rosalie and Dove and right now we're winnin'. "Listen, don't call me no more. You call again I'll have my peeps pay yo pyscho ass a visit." Click. "Jeez girl, problems?" Dove asked. Walkin' past I plucked her ear. Don't play wit' me, play rummy so I can continue takin' yo money, okay. * Three hours later, Glenda and I split the pot; then bein' tha nice bitch I am, I whipped out homemade nachos and margeritas. Turned on my stereo, threw in a mix of new and oldies cause that's what I do. Donel Jones started croonin' and Rosalie jumped up. "Yes, that's my baby right there! Girl I'd suck his fione ass inside out!" Please, Rosalie couldn't suck a lemon seed through a Cheerio; and to prove it, I broke out some sexy games. Bananas, cherries wit' stem, straws and a few sunflower seeds minus the shell, and stack of truth or dare cards. Bloodstain started playin' and Dove jumped to her feet, my lips curled. If she ain't stop flingin' fish round my apartment! "A'ight lets do this. Everybody grab a banana." Dove, Glenda and Rosalie picked one up. "You ain't playin'?" Questioned Rosalie. "Chile, if I enter, won't be no contest; so I'll sit this one out." Dove rolled her eyes; that's strike one. "Okay, lets see y'all dick suckin' and throatin' skills ladies." Each got to peelin'. Dove teased the tip wit' her tongue, Glenda licked up and down tha sides while Rosalie stuck half in her mouth and gagged, amaetuer. Dove leaned her head back and started slowly slidin' banana down her throat, Rosalie sneakily bit off a chunk, then tried again and Glenda's eyes watered as she tried takin' it all. Well damn, how these hoes please they men? It sure ain't wit' their oral skills that's for damn sure. Havin' seen enough, I moved on to the cherries and had each try and to tie a knot in tha stem. Again I sat out cause, I'ma pro boo. I can twist it up into two wit' no problem; ask 'bout me. This time Glenda won which surprised me, 'cause I taught Dove that move. Just goes to show, you can't teach a dumb hoe new tricks. Bitch so dumb she thinks Hamburger Helper comes wit' another person. She so dumb, she'll try and put M&M's in alphabetical order. I'm just sayin'. Whippin' out four seeds and straws, I decided to show these broads how it's done. Placin' straw over sunflower seed, I easily sucked it up, then stuck out my tongue to show 'em how it's done. Pow! How ya like me now? Rosalie won that round, she jumped up and started bumpin' and grindin' in celebration.

"Okay, okay, who's up for a lil truth or dare?" "Hell yeah, I love that game." squealed Glenda. "I wanna go first!" I ain't have a problem wit' it, so Glenda went first. "Rosalie, truth or dare?" "Truth." "How old were you when you gave it up? Who was he? And was it good?" A dreamy look slid across her face. "Oh my gosh, was it! His name was Donald Black; I was fourteen he was sixteen. It hurt like hell, but after a few strokes, I was hungry for more." Glenda giggled. "Somebody do me next." Rosalie grabbed a card, beatin' Dove to tha cards. "Have you done anal? If so how many times?" "Wait, you didn't say truth or dare." laughed Glenda. "Truth." Rosalie laughed and repeated tha question while I refreshed drinks. "Hmm, I think it was Johnny Joyner." "Cheater it's not think, truth or dare." chided Rosalie. "Okay, okay it was Johnny and I don't care for anal, I've only done it three times." "What!" yelled Dove like it was her hole bein' discussed. "Honey, anal is all that and then some. You've gotta relax. If its done right, you'll be in paradise." Dove picked up a card. "Tay', truth or dare?" "Dare." That's right, I ain't tellin' dese nosy mafuckas my business so they can spread it like fluff a nutta. I'm just sayin'. "I dare you to tongue kiss Rosalie." "Ooo!" Glenda loudly let out. Please, everybody done kissed a chick at one time in their life and if they deny it, they're lyin'. Standin', I pulled Rosalie to her feet, pulled her in and tongued her better than she's ever been tongued before. Ole girl started moanin' and breathin' hard. Pullin' away, I watched Rosalie slowly lick her lips before openin' her eyes. That's right boo, savor tha flavor. I know them panties drenched boo, too bad yo ass will always wonder every time you see me, bam! How ya like Taylor now! *

CHAPTER 19

I'm baack! And bat wings and syrup it's hot as hell in Atlanta! I don't see how a mafucka can breathe in this muggy ass weather, okay. Anyhoo, I checked into the Hilton which was two miles from Dr. Crawford's office, took a shower and was ready to pop my new booty. My appointment was scheduled for ten in the morning and if things went well, which I knew they would, I'd be under the knife ASAP; fuck waitin' weeks n shit. Dressed in a light yellow halter dress and sandals; keepin' it cute cause doin' more in this heat I'd probably melt. I bounced into tha lobby and asked concierge what was poppin' but not too far of a walk. Dude ran down a list long as my damn arm! I chose tha World of Coca-Cola museum and tha Center for puppetry arts. Hmp, I wasn't even payin' attention to tha little blonde white girl givin' tha tour, too busy rubber neckin' at all the possibilities walkin' by. Holey Batman drawers! Tha ATL know its got some fione, sexy, ding a lings down here! Lawda mercy! These nigga gone have me feelin' dicks in passin' and offerin' up blow job lunch specials 'cause my throats parched! I'm just sayin'. "Excuse me." a deep voice drawled that southern twang as he lightly tapped bare shoulder causin' goosebumps to race down my back, caress an ass cheek and anus to pucker. Turnin', I damn near drooled. Ole boy was finer then Tyson Beckford; could be his damn twin! Lawd let all these muscles lead to a nice sized pecker he can wield like a pile driver; carry me boo like Ving in Baby Boy. Amen. "Yes, can I help you?" I asked while thinkin', I sure can help you boo. I'll rock, roll and bounce all over yo ass, have you mutterin' gibberish, okay. "I think you dropped this." he held one of them business cards. Takin' it, I read the name Alex Lowery, optometrist. "Uh, no, its not mines." "It is now, I'm Alex and you are?" Ooo dis nucca's slick! "Taylor, nice to meet you." Umm, it's nice to meet you too boo, and it'll be even better when we're naked and sweatin' I'm just sayin'. "Atlanta's new to you hunh?" He smiled showin' off pearly whites and a small gap. Tha better to tease and suck my clit my dear, damn, its hot! "Yeah, just visitin'. How'd you know?" Alex licked his lips, "Your accent." I smiled. "Well since you're from here, where and what should I see while here?" Hint. Hint. "How about dinner, some dancin' and me on top of you?" Wait..what? "Excuse me." Alex stepped closer, tha scent of Giorgio engulfin' me. "I said, dinner, dancin' and me on top of you." Aww sukey now! Say whatchu feel boo and live up to it too gotdamnit! Cause I'm tired of nuccas comin' wit' game they can't even half damn deliver on okay. Quit wit' tha 'I'm packin' ten, insides damagin' inches' when yo ass carryin' round a fuckin' Kit Kat bar, okay. Stop stickin' out cha tongue talkin' 'bout 'I eat pus', I'll have yo ass climbin' walls.'. Hell yeah I'm climbin', to get away from yo teeth munchin' on my clit like it's a piece of steak. Quit wit' tha 'suck dis python' but when yo jeans drop I'm searchin' fo' yo python but all I see is lion dick. Three inches, okay; so don't do me boo, I ain't tha one okay. Big smile. "So you say, how do I know you can deliver?" Alex placed my hand smack on his zipper, uncarin' that people milled to and fro. Okay, but what I felt ain't mean shit, 'cause dudes been known to wear socks n shit for added girth and length. "I'm on my way back to the office, make sure you use the card so my actions can back up my words." Ooo, let me find out I done found my match out here. With a nod and few words of agreement, I got back to tha tour, my thoughts on Mr. Alex. Okay, I'm gonna skip all tha getting' to know you over dinner crap and get right to it, cause mafuckas in Atlanta got some serious damn issues. So Alex and I meet up in tha Hilton's lobby where he rented a room four floors below mines. I couldn't stop my eyes from caressin' bowed, hairy calves as we rode up on tha elevator. And when tha bell dinged and tha doors slid open, I wanted to race his ass to tha door. Walkin' in I took notice of bucket of ice chillin' a bottle of Clarke Bordeaux red. I ain't a wine drinker, fuck feelin' nice, a bitch likes getting' turnt ya heard. Reachin' up, I untied tha material around my neck, allowin' my dress to slither around my feet. "Damn, your flawless." I know boo, now let me see whatchu workin' wit'. As if he heard my thoughts Alex pulled his shirt up and off and my mouther watered. I love a man wit' that cobra back and across his was a lion's head, its mane blowin' in tha wind. Yess lawd, so far so good! Wigglin' outta thong, I dangled it from my finger, then sling shot it in his direction where it landed by his feet. Alex growled, scooped it up and gave tha crotch a tongue lick. That's what I'm talkin' 'bout, get warmed up boo for tha main course. I'm gonna have yo ass hooked, I'm just sayin'. Ten inches sprang to attention, jackpot! Even if Alex couldn't hang I'd still get mines wit' a package like that. So, we hop in bed right, Alex spreads my thighs and dives in. That tongue of his workin' my body oh so right, next thing I know I'm coatin' his tongue wit' sweetness which he gobbled up. He grabs a condom and I'm like good cause who knows what his freaky butts up to. I wince a lil as thickness nudges and stretches its way inside. Hell yeah, give momma that death stroke. And he did, we had tha headboard bangin' a tune accompanied by skin slappin' and moans of pleasure. So tha bed dips, but I'm not payin' that shit no mind, when I hear Alex hiss "Damn bae, that feels so good." My eyes fly open and I'm starin' at a pair of blue eyes. Tha fuck! Dudes atop Alex slidin' dick up his ass! Aww hell naw! Kinda freaky, deaky fuck fest is this?! Tha sound of balls slappin' ass had me ready to hurl, fuck feelin' good a minute ago, now tha switch's on and I'm ready to flip. Alex pounded, grabbin' my legs an puttin' 'em on his shoulders. Dude pounded Alex then started suckin' and lickin' my toes, Alex nibbled and bit my nipples, sendin' shards of pleasure shootin' straight to tha va jay jay. No way can I shove two full grown men off me, so I'm like fuck it and started talkin' cash shit like, 'Fuck dis pus' and give Alex all tha dick' ha! And when it was all over, disgusted or not, I got mines like I said I would. * Dr. Crawford's was busy as fuck wit' steady ringin' phones, patients comin' in and out and barely anywhere to fuckin' sit, after receivin' a bunch of forms to fill out. All types of people sat waitin'; saggy breasts, loose skin, huge discolored bags under tha eyes and more. I know one thing, I better be called in on time, or it's gone be some shit, I o'nt care how many partners up in here or if he's runnin' late. Paper work done, I stood to give it back to tha receptionist or whateva she was, when a door opened and my name was called. Smile bright, I followed some chick who said her name was Nancy like I gave a fuck, unless her ass was Dr. Crawford in disguise, to tha back. Nancy checked blood pressure, my weight and asked for a urine sample to verify if I was or wasn't pregnant. Chile please, pregnant. Tha thought was like starin' at Freddy in a locked room, no smank you! Five minutes later, there he was.... Dr. Crawford; lookin' gooder than a bitch on E in a room full a big bags of dope. Just fine for no damn reason; so fine all you can do is stare cause train of thought... gone. "Good morning." he greeted, voice all silky smooth. Ump, ump, ump! Tha things I could do, plus some I'd make up along tha way. "Mornin'." Jeezus I beg give me strength not to jump off this exam table and jump his bones. Amen. "So what brings you here today?" I swear I heard, 'do me here.'. Ooo chile I need some air, some water, somethin'. "I want a butt lift and after doin' my homework, you're the man to see, so here I am; all the way from CT." He smiled, panties creamin' okay. "Really, well thank you. Okay I'm gonna step out. Change into the gown so I can examine you and we'll go from there." Chile I ain't neva strip so fast. I almost bussed my ass comin' outta my damn thong. A knock and he was back, along wit' my blood pressure shootin' up when he checked out tiny cakes. "Well, there are two ways we can do this.."

Honestly I ain't hear much after 'we can do this' 'cause I was already figurin' out what I'd be wearin' afterwards. Dr. Crawford gave me a surgery date two weeks away; but after I bitched and moaned about how high my hotel bill would be, he scheduled it for two days from today. Yes! Nice ass, here I come! *

CHAPTER 20

Damn. Ass surgery hurts like a mafucka okay. Tha upside, tha pain meds and Dr. Crawford promptly returnin' my calls and soundin' so concerned. I can't lie, well I can, but I ain't right now. Anyway, some of them calls I made just so I could talk to his sexy self. Oh yeah, and Alex's freak McNasty behind called and left a message apologizin' in one breath and invitin' me for round two in another. Don't get me wrong, I'm up fo' just about anything; but be honest boo, don't be stashin' extra dick that ain't tag teamin' me okay. Shit, his ass sounded like ole blue eyes (Alex wouldn't share his name) was workin' wit' tha magic stick a'ight. Yeah I got mines, but hello! I'm called freak fo' a reason okayy and that's 'cause I like all holes plugged boo; fuck a finger okay. I'm just sayin'. * Six days after my surgery Dr. Crawford said I was all good and could go home or wait a lil longer. Uh..no, I'm outta this hot ass, hide in tha closet town. Three hours pass that and an additional four hundred and I was in tha air squeezed between an old chick who looked dead instead a sleep and some dude peckin' away on his laptop while cursin' under his breath. Ooo when tha plane touched down I got my strut on wit' a booty roll, shake and bounce. Somebody whistled, gassin' me up even more. Dese hoes really 'bout to hate!   * The next day I rolled up at Omaire's after drawin' straws on whom could tap it first, Omaire was the winner. Omaire had a bunch of company I noticed while parkin' and makin' my way to tha door which stood slightly open. Walkin' in, there were people everywhere, all wit' drinks in hand. After getting' my search on, I found Omaire out by tha pool. Oh shit, I had stumbled into one of Omaire's orgy parties. "T..Tay', w..how long y..you b..been here?" Omaire stuttered after spottin' me and walkin' over. "Hey boo. I was out and about and decided to stop by and show you this." Bam! A twirl and plump curvy cakes were in his face, surrounded by skin tight jeans I had to grease up wit' baby oil to slide into. His jaw dropped. "Nice, r..real n..nice." "So whats goin' on, whats all this?" "Its my boy Vance's comin' h..home party. He j..just came h..home from doin' s..six big ones." Big ones! Ah no boo, you blink and that shits over. Let me hear 'bout some Fed time, then we can talk, okay. "W..why d..don't you put on a b..bikini, show off t..that new b..booty." Oh hell yeah, I'm wit' it. Omaire always kept brand new swim wear on deck for those unprepared; so wit' a wink I headed inside. All kinds of one piece and two piece bikini sets hung on hangers a few wit' cute lil wrap arounds. I fingered a few price tags just to get an idea of how much Omaire was spendin' on a suit he most likely wouldn't see again and my eyes widened in disbelief. Six hundred and twenty-five for an Emilio Pucci one piece, seven hundred and ninety for Zahra. I snort. I don't think so, not when my cousin China's gurl Cha-Cha can get her sew on wit' five bucks worth of material, fifty bucks and a bottle of Henny and Cha-Cha will hook you up! Grabbin' a Norma Kamali Jorge wit' embellished green that appeared damn near see through, I got my pose on in tha full length mirror, snapped a few flicks for tha book so hoes can hate and strutted out to tha pool for some new possibles. After all a girl can never have to many. * Arrivin' home I was tired and sore, guess it was a lil to soon for all that twerkin' and grindin' I was doin', otha than that, I had a ball. Soon as I step in and close tha door somebody knockin'. I swear ninjas can't focus without my damn input or help, I'm just sayin'. "What!?" I snapped before I could even get tha damn door open good. Some chick who lived across tha street stood on my stoop lookin' all kinds of crazy. "Hey Tay' got a minute?" Whoa, first who tha hell are you? Whats yo name again, cause I barely pay yo ass any mind when I see you up at Blue's package store suckin' dick for bus tokens. "Sure, sup?" Ole girl whipped out a cute ass Mirkin crocodile bag, five-hundred-dollar price tag still danglin'. "I copped dis today, I know you like tha fly gear, so I came to see how much you'd give me for it." "Whats yo name again?" "Michelle, but every body calls me Micki, so do you want it?" Did a monkey scratch his ass on a tree? Hell yeah I wanted it, but I ain't offerin' shit boo, that's not how its done in tha world of boostin' okay; so come wit' a price, lets haggle or take yo ass on okay. "How much?" "Four hundred." she rushed out, then started fidgetin'. Ooo its tha old fien need a hit game. "Nah I'm good." I made to close tha door. "Wait! I..I mean three seventy five." "Nah, that's still a lil steep." Add in some arm clawin' to go wit' that fidgetin'. "Okay, okay, uh....three hundred that's as low as I can go." she whined like I give two cow balls. "Two seventy-five is all I have." sigh. "Okay, deal." Containin' a smile I quickly reached in my pocket (never put money in yo purse okay, cause yo ass askin' to get jacked) counted out two hundred and seventy-five bucks and passed it, ole Micki looked pissed. "Thought you said you only had two seventy-five. I clearly saw more than that in yo hand." Yo fault for countin' my money, key word boo, mines, you live to steal anotha day and learned a valuable lesson, class dismissed.

"Do you want yo bag back?" I asked. Even thought I ain't givin' her ass shit but tha door closin' in her fucked up face, I'm just sayin'. "Naw, naw, I..." I closed tha door, like I always say, I can't stand a scary bitch. How yo ass sellin' somethin' and can't even talk right? Hoe please, gone get cho crack, smoke and fry up tha rest of yo cells so I can clean yo ass out of yo items on tha next go round. Thank you, come again! *

CHAPTER 21

Hmp, I'm back at work and that lil dude's in charge cause Hex's ass is out of town, so he's followin' me around so close I can feel his breath on my ass, syke, but tha nuccas close and pesterin' tha shit outta me, fo' really real. "What!?" I snapped after Larry Love cornered me by coat check, tha switch jiggled. "So when we gonna hook up Tay'? I been patiently waitin'." Patient hunh, every other day dudes textin' me bullshit smiley faces, thinkin' of you's or askin' me where and what I like to eat. Dick nigga, that's what I like to eat A1 Prime Cut, I like it well seasoned boo, where it melts in my mouth and in my hands okay. I'm just sayin'. So don't do me cause I got cramps and I ain't in tha mood. "You always brushin' a brotha off, what I gotta do to get half tha attention you be givin' these corny ass niggas up in here." Ooo dis lil midget tryin a take me there. Nucca I'm grown, well pass tha age of let a nucca tell me what to do. I can have a thousand as he said corny niggas

171

in my face and still not give yo ass tha time of day until I fuckin' feel like it. "Oh word, that's how you feelin'?" "Hell yeah, now I see why broads end up alone or dogged out, ya'll play to many games." he women bashed. Ooo he done it now, switch flipped and it was on. "Broad? First off, get some knowledge boo. Don't be mad cause no females give you tha time of day. You to eager boo, too desperate. You're like an annoyin' ass fly buzzin' tha same shit over and over in my damn ear. And so fuckin' what we haven't hooked up, I'ma busy bitch boo; so take a number and wait yo turn. Second Taylor Janae James ain't neva ever been dogged out. I dog niggas okay and third, I choose to be alone boo, so I can do me without annoyin' fly's in my ear questionin' where I been and who I'm fuckin' and otha dumb shit, you must be fienin' boo. Its okay, you ain't tha first and definitely won't be tha last. You wanna know what you can do to get some play, ain't that whatchu said? Hmm, how 'bout grow nigga, I feel like I'm talkin' to a twelve-year-old, buy some shoe lifts boo, or get like Prince and rock some heeled boots okay. Heres another tip, stop bathin' in Giorgio, that's what soap and waters for okay. Ass smells good one minute and like ass tha next!" Bam! Larry's jaw twitched, I wish a nigga would, his ass betta act like he know. "Fuck you." Well damn, is that all he's got? I laughed and walked over to tha bar, cause now I need a damn drank. * Dove walked across freshly cut grass and smiled. Things were comin' along nicely, she stared at three painters settin' up around tha buildin', ready to paint it her favorite colors, purple and grey, tomorrow tha pavers would arrive to re-do tha driveway. Soon Taylor..soon. * An hour later, back in her apartment, Dove went over plan A and B again and again, tryin to ignore tha whispers goin' on inside her head. Yesterday her shrink's office had left a message requestin' she call and make an appointment or they'd be forced to alert her legal guardian that she hadn't been seen in months; nor had she re-filled any of her medications. "Shut up!" Dove clapped hands over her ears as her mothers harpin' seemed to get louder and louder. "Dove Denise Mitchell! I know you hear me you good for nothing little bitch!" Yelled Connie Mitchell, Dove's mother. At age eight, she was terrified of her mother and the punishments she wielded. Shaking those thoughts away, Dove quickly dialed Dr. Michael's office to set up an appointment, she needed to be free to bring her plan to fruitition. * "Its good to see you Dove." said Dr. Michael's. "How have you been?" "Fine." muttered Dove, eyes on her twiddlin' fingers. "Have you been taking your medication I prescribed?" Her eyes shot up. "I don't need any medication. Besides, I don't like the way it makes me feel." Dr. Michael's nodded, grey eyes alit from the joy of helping others. "Asshole." Dove murmured, not carin' if Dr. Michael's heard her. "Tell me Dove, are you still hearing voices?" Dove stiffened. 'Omg! How

much longer do we have to sit here listenin' to this gobbily gook!'
Yelled her alter persona Megan who she hadn't heard from in
years. "Uh..no..well..sometimes I hear my mother, yellin',
screamin', at me." "And how does that make you feel now that
you're an adult?" 'Don't ansa dis cracka Dove! He's bein' real
damn nosy.' Argued Megan. "Dove. Can you answer the
question?" Throat suddenly dry, Dove swallowed a few times,
tryin' to work up enough saliva to coat dry throat. "W..what did
you ask me?" "Dove I'd like to have you admitted at the Institute
of Living for a few days.." "No! I mean no Dr. Michael's, I'm
fine, that's not necessary. Um, I'll start takin' my medication....I
promise." Dr. Michael's opened desk draw and withdrew a
couple of samples he'd placed there for just this reason. Dove
stared at the three samples, Paliperdone, Prolixin and Zoloft,
then reached out and swiped them off his desk. "I'll get you
some water." "Water? Why do I need water?" She asked confused.
"I'd like you to take them now, that way by the time you reach
home they should be working. Of course you'd need to take
them everyday for it to be effective." 'Just do it so we can leave
already!' Megan ordered. "Okay." Dove quickly tore open the
samples which held eighteen pills in all. Dr. Michael's handed
her a cup of water, Dove popped all three, sipped some water,
swallowed, then opened her mouth and lifted her tongue to
show she'd swallowed them. "Make sure you pick up your

medication from the pharmacy." * "Damn gurl why you bein' so anti?" Glenda asked of Dove who'd been mia for days. Dove listlessly stared at Glenda before allowin' her inside. Glenda stepped in and frowned, Dove's place was spotless! Eyes wide, Glenda took in sticky free floors and a couch free of clothin'. "Whats tha occasion? 'Cause you and cleanin' are allergic to each other." she joked, then flopped on tha couch and lit up a cigarette. "So whats good, whatchu up to?" Dove sat beside Glenda, swiped her cigarette and inhaled. "Nothin' much, just chillin', gettin' my thoughts together. Sup over in tha Courts?" "Whoo, drama as always; that Micki chick got stomped out by mom dukes, she's on drugs heavy and been stealin' any and everythin'. Supposedly she sold Tay' an expensive bag, oh and Shelly's in jail. Her mom had her arrested for stealin' her disability check." Dove snorted. "Did Tay' give tha bag back?" Before Glenda could answer, Dove started back talkin'. "Of course she didn't, cause she's queen Taylor." "Okay, lets keep it real, we both know we wouldn't have returned that bag either. So again, tell me why you act like you can't stand Taylor, but your always in her face." Dove jumped up and begin pacin'. "Tell me why everyones so team Taylor? She ain't nuttin' special damn, stop ridin' her ass!" Spewed Dove. "Speakin' of ass, girl Taylor done got that booty she'd been sayin' up for." Glenda added like she didn't just hear Dove ventin'. Teeth grindin' put

Glenda on pause. "Wait, your serious?" "Fuck yeah, I can't stand her know it all ass." "Okayy, then why be around her? Help me understand, I mean did she steal yo man, get you arrested..?" "I don't need a reason, just know I always keep my enemies close and you'd be wise to do tha same." *

CHAPTER 22

"Got a minute?" asked Larry Love. Dove, out of breath from workin' stage and floor coldly grilled him. "What nigga?" Dove nastily replied. She'd heard tha other girls complainin' about Hex's boy; that he'd been caught jackin' off while watchin' tha girls strip through a hole he'd put in tha wall, to harassin' tha girls on performin' sexual acts. Just a straight perv. "Relax, don't nobody want yo worn out pussy. If you ain't in tha rooms suckin' for a buck, yo ass leavin' tha club fuckin' for one." snapped Larry. "Hex wants to see you." He finished, shot tha bird and kept it movin'. 'Fuck', thought Dove. Bein' all doped up she'd totally forgotten stealin' from Hex and now here she was bein' led to slaughter because medication had her slippin', badly. Takin' a deep breath, Dove straightened her spine and headed for Hex's office. Dove knocked, opened tha door and stepped in, 'Fuck waitin' for a come in, when I'm on tha way out'. Thought Dove.

Hex sat behind a massive marble desk; its surface covered with papers, telephone, computer, a rolodex and more. Two wood cabinets sat against one wall, a mini bar on another, pictures of the usual ghetto fuckery adorned the walls; a dog playin' poker, a naked black velvet beauty wit' afro. "Close the door." Hex ordered. Dove did as told; crossed the room and stood before his desk petulant look in place, arms crossed. "You wanted to see me." Hex cued up somethin' on tha computer, then swiveled it in her direction. Her eyes snapped wide, there she was, naked and searchin' through dresser drawers, and again sittin' naked on his bed, greedily thumbin' through a stack in hand. "You got anythin' you'd like to say?" "I was puttin' it back Hex. I know it was wrong, but I really really needed it." Dove hastily shot out, then licked dry lips. "Why didn't you come to me?" Cold eyes froze her in place, the urge to pee suddenly squeezed her bladder. "Hex," Dove timidly whispered, "I've really gotta pee, I promise to answer all your questions, if I can just use your bathroom, please." Hex waved his hand and Dove took off, stepped inside Hex's personal bathroom and gasped. Heated flooring, a frosted glass shower, heated towel racks. Racing to tha toilet, Dove lowered tha seat, hiked up skirt, yanked down thong, plopped down and released a steady stream of pee. Done, Dove flushed, fixed her clothes, bypassed tha sink and soap and re-entered Hex's office. "You were sayin'?" Dove exhaled. "I needed tha money. I only took seventy-five thousand, and so far I've put back five. As soon as my investment pays off I'll pay you tha rest, I promise." Unreadable eyes watched her every move, every expression. "What kinda investment? I hope it ain't some lame." "Please, don't insult me. Hell no I didn't invest seventy-five thousand on no worthless ass nigga." Hex chuckled. "You got courage, I like that." A gun appeared atop his desk. "But right now, I want a lil fear; maybe a smidgen of courage while you spill tha truth, otherwise...." Hex chambered a round, "now whats it gone be." "I'm gonna open a hoe house, that's why I needed the money, please don't shoot me." Pleaded Dove. "A hoe house hunh?" Dove shook her head so fast she got dizzy and had to grab the desks edge to keep from tumbling to the floor. Hex stood, stuck gun in his back waistband, then came around the desk, stopping when he stood behind Dove, raised his hands and rested them atop her shoulders. "I want in. You do that and I'll take a loss on the fifteen and call it even." He said, as he started massaging her shoulders.....hard. Dove winced and relunctly agreed. * Got damn! This ass of mines is attractin' niggas left and right, like a damn magnet! Babyy soon as I step outside they start flockin', pullin' over and yellin', buyin' everythin' I had on tha counter in tha store. One mafucka handed over seven hundred dollars, one had his cell written on 'em. I'm like okayy, I see you boo, ballin! Fuck if I can remember his damn name though, so I put him in my phone as 'the seven hundred-dollar man.' Smirk. Anyhoo, I'm gone go kick it wit' my handicap boo Ty, see if tha dick's still good; okay. Brandon and now Joshua were constantly callin' and textin' but ain't shit happenin' unless I decide different, ya heard. Ty opened tha door, lookin' kinda sexy for someone in a wheelchair; wearin' Escada jeans and a green top, Nikes on his feet. "Hey boo, you lookin' all sexy, where you goin' to see wifey and tha kids?" That's right, Ty was married wit' two lil bad ass sons. His wife said she couldn't take tha stress of bein' wit' him and hauled ass. So how can we get married you ask? We ain't and not cause his ass already married and claimin' to be in tha process of divorcin', but cause I ain't neva doin' that shit again. Plus, I still love my husband who I have no urge to divorce. "I just got back. Deloris bein' her usual bitchy self." "Aww." I leaned down and slipped him some tongue. "Want me to beat dat ass boo?" Ty rubbed his jaw. "I might, its five thou in it for you." "Done." Even though he'd said maybe, fuck all tha extras. Ty laughed, "You be wildin' ma." "Sure do and you love every minute of it." Ty reached around and squeezed an ass cheek only for his eyes to widen in pleasant surprise. "Damn ma, I like." Gigglin' I took a seat on his lap. "I'm horny bae, can you help me wit' that?" I whined like a lil kid, then bit my lip. "Hell yeah." Turnin', Ty wheeled us down tha hall and into his bedroom. Aww shit, Ty done upgraded to a big ass Cali king bed. I can't wait to work his ass atop it. Standin' up, I started windin' and strippin'; by the time I was naked, Ty's snausage was tentin' his dress slacks. "Ooo somebody's horny..I mean happy to see me." Ty pulled his shirt up and off, revealin' he was back on his workout regime. Walkin' over to tha bed I bounced on it, testin' its firmness. Ty eased himself from chair to bed where I happily helped him from sneaks, slacks and boxers. Dick stood at attention, salutin' a 'hey how you doin',' my answer, a nice long, slow lick. Ty moaned, so I gave a few more licks, a kiss or two, then dived in; swallowin' til' nose met hairs. "Sshit!" hissed Ty, toes ballin'. I know boo, you can buss 'cause I know you want to. "Mmm." hummin' had fists clenchin' tha sheets while his eyes slammed closed and his mouth fell open. Cheeks cavin', I sucked that pop til' creamy fillin' erupted down my throat. Ty was breathin' all hard as I drained him dry and kept goin' til' he was back rock hard and rarin' to go. Seconds later, I climbed aboard reverse cowgirl and rode that buckin' bronco to tha finish line. * Later that day I went by Pope Park and hung out wit' tha Puerto Ricans. Ty had willingly given up all info on where Deloris hung out. She lived up tha street from tha park and usually went everyday to have a few beers while waitin' to scoop Darren and Danny from school. Only cause I like Ty would I give her ass a pass, since she'd be on her way to pick 'em up. But tomorrow was another day. * Hex walked around the property with Dove listening to her plans to open a hoe house. "You can come up wit' tha name Hex, cause I'm stumped." Hex smiled. "A'ight, let me think on it." "Okay, so what do you think 'bout tha place so far?" "I like it, when will the inside be ready?" He asked. "Probably another month. I need to round up some women too." said Dove. "No prob', I know a few peeps that'd be happy as hell to get off the streets and work in a safer environment." "And how much should I..I mean we charge 'em?" Hex pondered the question a moment. "On the street a trick gotta put in long hours to make that quota. We definitely need to charge more than fifty for a dick suck; that's for damn sure. C'mon let's head back to my place and come up with some prices." Dove smiled wide. "Anythin' you say daddy." she cooed. *

CHAPTER 23

Today was Dove's b-day. Tha ole hag's been mia a lot and actin' kinda shady, so me and Glenda decided to pop up on that ass to see whats shakin'. Pullin' up, we saw tha usual stuntin' ass, broke usin' chicks for a place to lay ninjas outside drinkin', smokin' and talkin' shit to every chick strollin' past. Here it is September, fall 'bout to roll in and you ain't got shit better to do than harass a bitch cause she ain't tryin a upgrad yo tired ass. I'm just sayin'. Glenda knocked, only for tha door to swing open. "Ah uhn, I'll wait for you outside. You know black people don't fare well in situations like these" Glenda uttered in a high tone of voice. I grabbed her arm, haltin' any chance of escape. "Girl, cut it out, you don't hear no spooky music cause this ain't a horror flick. Now bring yo ass." I told her, then yanked her right on inside. My eyes widened in shock, someone done come in and tore her shit up! One couch was all slashed tha hell up, her coffee table lay smashed, even tha TV she fucked tha Aarons manager for was totaled. "The fuck?" whispered Glenda, eyes wide in fright. "Ow bitch! Stop diggin' yo damn cat paws in my arm!" I yelled, switch jigglin'. "Sorry, sorry." repeated Glenda, slowly trudgin' for tha kitchen. "Fuck you goin'?" Glancin' at me over her shoulder, Glenda said, "To get a stiff drank. I gotta feelin' I'ma need it." Dis bitch right here! I swear if I'm ever in trouble and a mafucka send scary, chicken I'ma go ham. I could hear cabinets open and close, followed by ice cubes droppin' into glass, then the fridge. When she appeared she had one of them Big Gulp cups in hand. Damn lush, I'm just sayin'. "You ready now, or you need to go whip up a ham samich?" Half smile on her face, Glenda took a few sips and said, "I'm ready." Scoopin' a coffee table leg as we passed, we started down tha hall, steppin' on mashed potatoes and Salisbury steak which Glenda slipped and fell in. Tha shit was funny cause her ass ain't spill a drop out that Big Gulp I betcha. "Girl get tha hell up. Good googily moogily, maybe you should've waited outside." That hoe nodded, turned and made like she was gone wait outside. "Not today hoe, so turn right tha fuck around. Don't make me read you hunny cause nows not tha time, but I can always serve a quickie." I told her ass right quick. Glenda froze, turned, stuck them dick suckas out and whined, "I don't wanna die Tay'. Lil Marvin's only eight, he needs me, please let me wait outside, that way if shit goes left, I can call 911." Her crazy behind sang, like she was Wyclef and I was Mary, cause ain't no way I'm that fugly bastard okay; and I heard he's Haitain. Ump, he's givin' Haitains a bad rap out here thinkin' he's tha shit and aint had a hit since Kione was born. Oh snap, focus Taylor, focus. I felt like I was in a scene from tha Wizard of Oz when its dark and they're skippin' down tha yellow brick road. Fuckin' Glenda done wrecked my damn nerves. Reachin' in my purse I grabbed mace and brass knuckles; ignorin' Glenda's pleas to let her hold somethin'. Fuck I look like boo? If you ain't got no protection you better throw them hands. I'm just sayin'. "Open tha door." Glenda eyed me like I was crazy before swallowin' and doin' as told. Tha bathroom door stood open and empty, except for tha shredded shower curtain and towel racks, torn from tha wall. Glenda started hyperventilatin' so I started towards Jeff's room. "Wait. Please don't leave me!" Glenda's gonna get a smack I swear to gawd. Tha switch's gonna flip if this fool don't stop yankin' on my got damn Ellesse top; I'm just sayin' cause this top ain't cheap, okay. "Sorry, I know you're probably sick of hearin' that.." "You damn right I am. Now pull it together before I clock yo ass one good time." Mouth open to apologize, Glenda thought about it, then quickly snapped it shut. Jeff's room was a mess, bed overturned, mattress and box spring destroyed, dresser drawers smashed. "Good God what tha hell is Dove into?" Questioned Glenda.

Right. But now wasn't tha time for twenty damn questions of guess what tha slore did now okay. Soon as we reached Dove's room, Glenda squealed, "Oh my God, did you hear that?" Then clasped a hand over her mouth, though she didn't spill a drop outta that damn cup. She wasn't even sippin' on it. "Hear what? I ain't here shit, 'cause you can't shut cho trap for five seconds. If someone is in there they know we out here." I snapped, Glenda gulped, then guzzled from her cup. I swung tha door open and sighed in relief at not findin' Dove's dead body splayed out across tha floor. "See, Dove ain't even here," I said, right before Glenda, who was behind me, screamed. Whippin' round, my eyes damn near popped from their sockets at tha sight of a huge mafucka all in black includin' mask swingin' on Glenda. "Oh hell naw!" Jumpin' up, I swung brass knuckled fists, followed by an eyeful of mace. He bellowed like a wounded bear. Before I could continue my assault, tha closet door opened and another big figure in all black jumped out, grabbed me from behind, and slapped a chloroform rag over my nose. Tha last thing I remembered was crumblin' to tha floor next to an unconscious Glenda......................

THE END

SNEAK PEEK

BEING YOUNG CAN BE DANGEROUS

COUGER

When Your Being Haunted

III

CHAPTER ONE

Damn, my head hurts. Groggy as hell, I slowly peeled my eyes open and watched the ceilin' spin. No, it's a ceilin' fan slowly rotating. Confused, I stared at it a moment, tryin' to remember what happened. Nothin' but poundin' temples. Slowly sittin' up, I looked dazedly around; plain white walls in a windowless room, that kinda looked like it used to be a storage closet. My foot kicked somethin' and my mouth dropped as a roll of tissue fell over and rolled towards a mop bucket. Tha fuck?! "Where tha hell am I?" Came out soundin' dry and raspy. Pullin' up to my feet, I walked over to a door, gripped knob and gave a twist, then again. Locked. Tha shit was locked! "Think Taylor, what's the last thing you remember?" I asked myself while leanin' against tha door. Bits and pieces ran through my mind like a freshly opened 500 piece puzzle poured on the table. I remembered Glenda comin' over 'cause she hadn't heard from Dove and was worried. I stiffened.

Glenda! I was wit' Glenda, was she here too? Another thought popped in, we'd gone over to Dove's; whom I thought was probably getting' banged by as many dicks as possible. Only, when we got there, Dove's place was trashed. And then what? Slammin' my eyes shut, I concentrated so hard I didn't even realize I'd moved until I ran into tha damn wall. "Ouch, fuck!" I would've kicked it but I didn't have on any shoes. My shoes! Them mafuckas cost me three hundred and fifty bucks on sale. Somebody was askin' for it! Okay, okay, focus Tay'; fuckin' focus. Throbbin' temples be damned, I needed to know where tha fuck I was and how I got here. Oh yeah, and where was Glenda and Dove. * I don't know how many hours I sat in that room/closet 'til I caved and used tha bucket to pee. Talk about humiliated, all I needed was a camera in my face recordin' my squat. Ooo, it's on when I find tha culprit; ain't gone be no fuckin' talkin'! Hungry and thirsty, I hope whoever did this hurries up and shows wit' some fuckin' nourishment before I waste away; losin' my shape in tha process. I wonder if anyone's lookin' for me, probably not. Which meant I'd have to help me myself. * Stomach growlin', throat dry, hands sore from poundin' against tha door; I lay curled in a ball fantasizin' 'bout layin' on a tropical island bein' catered to by a bunch of oiled up, buff, loin cloth wearin' gawds caterin' to my every whim. Tha shit was so real I swear I smelled chicken soup. My eyes snapped open in time to see a steamin' bowl bein' slid into the closet/room before tha door slammed closed. A lock clicked loudly in tha silence. Too weak to stand, I crawled over to said bowl, tossed tha spoon, picked up tha bowl and drank it down; chokin' on bits of chicken and noodles in my haste to put nourishment in my stomach. After awhile, I started namin' and singin' TV show theme songs to keep my sanity; like from Sanford & Son. Redd Foxx as Fred Sanford was hilarious and Kung Fu. Then I hummed tha Jefferson's which was another favorite, that Sherman Hemsley was pretty funny. Finally, tha door opened and in walked a behemoth of a man wearin' jeans, steel toed construction boots and tee shirt; his peanut shaped head void of hair. "Who are you? Where am I?" "Get up and put this on." he ordered, ignorin' my questions. Glancin' down, I saw he'd tossed me one a them eye masks people use to block out light when tryin' a sleep. "How 'bout no." Dude just stood there, like he's stuck on stupid waitin' on me. So I played tha waitin' game too. Fuck dat, I need to see where tha fuck I am. Dude sighed and said, "We can do this easy, where you walk on your own or I can knock yo ass out and carry you. Yo choice." Frownin', I sized his ass up right quick. At least six three, and bigger than Dwayne 'the Rock' Johnson and Ving Rhames put together; just too damn big for no reason. Damn dick probably shriveled to raisin status. I'm just sayin'. Crackin' ashy knuckles on hooves sized hands, dude snatched my collar, yanked me up and shook me so hard my brain rattled. Slappin' the eye mask on, I felt pain explode in my jaw before darkness claimed me. "Good, you're awake." said a voice I immediately recognized. Larry Love. I laughed. "Fucks so funny?" "You nigga. You that desperate where you had to snatch me up?" I snorted. "Fuckin' pitiful." I knew I sat tied to a chair, 'cause I could feel ropes bindin' my ankles and wrists. Suddenly tha mask was yanked off, followed by a hard slap. Blood tinged my lip so I licked it off. "Yum, what else you got?" Larry frowned. "That cocky game you playin' won't last long once you start yo new job." Smirked Larry, wishin' he had a camera to snap her face once he delivered the coup de gras. "If yo stupid ass don't untie me, tha first chance I get I'll slit yo fuckin' throat." I coolly told him, meanin' every word. Another slap. "Yeah, yeah. That won't be happening no time soon." Larry lit a Black & Mild, inhaled then blew smoke right in my face, the switch jiggled. "Ooh I'm so scared Taylor." Larry fake shivered. "Please don't kill me. I think you got it backwards, you'll be the one wishin' for death after a thousand or more niggas run all up in yo ass, bitch." A bad feelin' swept over me. "That's right bitch, welcome home. Welcome to The Dark Cavern hoe house."

CHAPTER TWO

I gave up on tryin' to figure out how long I'd been here and was now focused on findin' a way out. From closet/room to tied up in a chair, I still talked hella shit to Larry Love every time I saw his face. In his anger, he let it slip that I wasn't tha only one here; and that soon we'd all be sellin' our bodies for cash. I also found out I'd been there three weeks when I told Larry that someone would come lookin' for me. That bastard laughed so hard, tears ran down his face. It's all good, cause Taylor knows how to play too. I started yellin' and screamin'. My ass is sick of this fuckin' chair, I'm hungry and though I hate to admit it, I stink to high heaven since I haven't touched water since snatched. I thought I heard someone else yellin' too, but I wasn't sure. Tha lock clicked and the door swung open, smackin' tha wall. I knew someone was there though no one said anythin'. Tuggin' at the rope around my ankles alerted me whoever it was had crossed tha floor. Then my hands were freed, so I automatically reached up to remove face mask; only to cry out in pain when two of my fingers were squeezed and bent back, damn near touchin' finger to knuckles I'm sure. "Ow! Okay, okay!" Hand throbbin' I awaited orders on what he or she wanted. A hand gripped my arm and tugged, so I stood up and was led from tha room. Minutes later, even though I struggled, four hands divested me of all clothin' and doused my ass wit' freezin' shower water. A bar of soap was slapped in one hand, a thin ass rag in another. I felt like dis chick name Courtney who used to live in Dove's building last summer, 'cause I couldn't see shit and had to rely on other senses. So far I learned besides Larry's ass, there was another man who always smelled of peppermint candy and two chicks. I knew this cause both them dyke bitches always copped feels, their hands were too soft to be a man's. Fuckin' hoes on my list too. "Time," a voice grunted, scarin' me from my thoughts. A rough ass towel was tossed in my face, shit felt like it was peelin' skin as I dried off. Bein' sneaky, I dried my face, liftin' tha mask slightly so I could get a glimpse of one of these hoes. Reba! Clenchin' teeth, I quickly stuck my arm out, towel in hand to let 'em know I'm done; while debatin' on whether I make a move now, or wait. Towel yanked from my grip, both captors took an arm and walked me naked a few paces before shovin' me in a room, then lockin' me inside. Snatchin' off mask, I took in eight twin beds, all empty; while one held bedding, a pair of shorts and a faded white tee shirt. Givin' a sniff, I slowly slid on tha shorts since no panties or bra were in sight, then pulled on tha shirt which was snug as hell. There were two windows; the inside covered by wire used in chicken coops, the outside by bars; that eliminated exit by window. Fuck! Nothin' on tha walls to use as a weapon, no lamp or table. The door unlocked; I jumped to my feet heart racin'. A young white girl, around maybe eighteen or nineteen wit' fiery red hair on head and snatch was shoved inside; followed by a rolled mattress, which unfurled as tha door closed, revealin' pillow, blanket and tha same outfit I wore. Wet hair dripped trails of water down her back where they raced each other towards an ass so flat I told myself once we made it out, I'd hook her up wit' Dr. Crawford's number. "Hey." she greeted; finally coverin' her 40C's and hairy cat. "Sup." I returned dryly, idly wonderin' what's her story. "I'm Hannah, what's your name?" "Tay'." Short and sweet boo, cause I ain't here to make friends. "Any idea where we are, or how we got here?" Damn, chatty Hannah! Don't chu see my ass on lock just like you? Fuck outta here. I thought. "Sorry, that was a stupid question." she said. Amen sista'. "I still don't know how I ended up here. One minute I'm at the bus station asking for change," Uh no boo, get it right, it's called beggin' okay. "And the next, I woke up locked in a storage closet." My ears perked up. "Do you remember who you spoke to before wakin' up here?" Hannah frowned a minute, then gave a wide smile like her answer would win her money on Jeopardy. "Yeah, yeah, I do. It was some black lady. She asked me was I a runaway, and if I was hungry. I told her yes, I'm from Wyoming. I'd run away from my abusive, rapist step father and sure, I could eat. She flashed a bunch of cash and offered to take me to...shit, I can't remember. Anyway, I got in the front seat, we pull off and someone pops up from the backseat; slapped a rag over my face and voila, here I am." Hannah scooped up mattress, pillow and blanket then chose the empty bed closest to mines. I hope dis air head don't think we 'bout to be tha best of fuckin' friends, just cause I asked her ass a question. 'Cause it ain't happenin' okay. Layin' down I stared at water stained ceilin' wonderin' if Glenda and Dove would be next to be shoved into tha room. "Psst, psst." My eyes shot open. Damn, I don't even remember fallin' asleep, but darkness had fallen. "What." I snapped, ready to flip tha script if her ass woke me for somethin' stupid. "Listen." A scream rang out. "Omg, you hear that?" Duh, hell yeah I hear that! Again a scream rang out. Since we had no lights, I didn't know Hannah was cryin' til I heard snifflin'. "Tha fuck is you cryin' fo'?!" I yelled. "Shut tha hell up befo' they hear yo crybaby ass and they come in here!" "Sorry....I'm sorry, I'm just so scared. Can I....can I get in bed wit' you....please?" Hannah loudly whispered. Rollin' eyes, I retorted wit' a, "Hell naw, fuck I look like. Now pull it togetha' fo' I smack the fuck out chu." The door swung open, hallway light spilled in tha room. Every time tha door opened my eyes would spring to our captor who always wore a ski mask, completely obliteratin' any chance of knowin' who they were. A muffled 'oompf' sounded when she was shoved in tha room so hard she crashed to tha floor; wackin' knees and elbows on tha hard linoleum. Hannah stumbled from bed, I guess to offer assistance to tha girl still lyin' on tha floor cryin'. My teeth ground togetha', cause I'm in a room wit' a buncha fuckin' crybabies I swear. Two shadows rose from tha floor just as the door opened and a rolled up mattress flew in, conkin' ole gurl in tha back. She in turn fell against Hannah and both went down. Fuckin' Three Stooges minus one, da fuck! Just before tha door closed I quickly asked, "Please, I beg you. May I have somethin' to drink?" Almost chokin' on my damn tongue to force it out soundin' all sugar and nice. Tha door slammed wit' no reply. Suckin' teeth, I flopped back in bed glad Hannah and whoever were quiet. Tha door opened and a small Styrofoam cup appeared. Shootin' from bed I almost bussed my ass on what felt like a piece of clothin'. "Thank you so much, bless you." Jeezus if I keep it up I'ma hurl big chunks. Takin' cup, the door closed, then locked. Since I couldn't see, I sniffed the cup, then took a cautious sip; memories of Dove spikin' my drink dancin' in my head. Orange juice, and it was nice and cold. Even so, I only took anotha' sip, then sat on my bed and waited to see what reaction I'd have before drinkin' anymore. "Tay' this is Sophie, she's eighteen and from Hartford as well." So. Fuck I look like, tha city takin' a census!? These bitches gone make tha switch flip and it ain't gone be pretty okay. 'Cause I gotta lotta tension I'm dealin' wit' and I don't have tha patience fo' tha bull. I'm just sayin'. Mornin' came grey and listless. I had to twist my frame all crazy just to see the sky through all tha crap blockin' tha window. The view was nothin' but grass and trees as far as tha eye could see. I couldn't even tell if this was tha front of the building or not. Hannah yawned, then stretched wit' a bunch of bones crackin'. "Mornin' Tay', Sophie." she greeted. "Sup," Hannah snorted. "You don't say much hunh?" Sophie rolled over, farted, then sat up, big owl like eyes focused on me. "I talk when I've got shit to say." Leavin' tha window I walked back over to my bed, bent and scooped up my orange juice. I'd left a drop in it last night, but this mornin' tha fuckin' cups bone dry. "A'ight let's get shit straight right damn now, if I have somethin' and don't offer to share, don't wait til I'm sleep to get sticky fingers, 'cause you'll get beat da fuck down!" I snapped, switch jigglin'. "Sorry, thought it was for all of us." said Sophie. I glared at this dumb bunny and flipped. "Listen here Sophie, did yo wailin' ass ask for a drink last night? No, 'cause you was too damn busy cryin'. Did Hannah ask? No. So how tha fuck you got share outta me bein' tha only one to speak up? I don't know nor care, all I know is you touch my shit again and it's yo ass, understand!?" I loudly exclaimed. Sophie stood, blinked and gone say, "Omg, it was barely a sip. Must you people always blow things way outta proportion." Ooo, no she didn't throw out tha 'you people' card. Droppin' cup, I marched right up in her space, hummin' breath and all. "Listen you redneck, backwoods, country, road kill eatin' bitch. You don't know me boo, you comin' at me like you want me to snatch yo ass one good time." I chest bumped her. "I dare yo ass to say anotha' word, racist or nah!" Sophie quickly glanced at Hannah so my head followed; 'cause we all know 'them people' stick togetha', but Hannah was still beside her bed. Before my head finished turnin', Sophie reached out and slapped me. Ballin' a fist, I returned her serve wit' a punch to them racist ass, juice drinkin' lips followed by anotha to an eye, then I shoved her ass. Tha back of her legs hit tha bed followed by Sophie fallin' on and off on the opposite side. Breathin' hard cause adrenaline's flowin' and I thought wit' all that mouth she'd give me some exercise. I glared at Sophie, picked up my cup and tossed it at her. Sophie lay on tha floor, cryin' like I'd attempted murder and she'd barely escaped. Hoe please. Dustin' my hands on lightweight, I strode back to my bed, peepin' how Hannah stared at me in awe. That's right boo, now you know Taylor ain't nothin' to fuck wit', no matter if it's orange juice or a fuckin' corner slice of bread.

CHAPTER THREE

This time after showers, we were givin' toothbrushes. Brushin' neva felt so good! One of tha guards asked Sophie what happened to her lip. I hadn't hit her hard enough to cause a black eye, but her lips were puffy like she'd just left from havin' collagen injections. I silently dared her ass to look my way or mutter my name. She's smarter than I thought cause she lied and said that it happened when tha guard pushed her in tha room last night. Then it was back to our room where breakfast waited on our beds, which consisted of two eggs, waffles, a boiled egg, two slices of bacon and a small pint of milk like they served at school lunch. Just to be funny, I demanded Sophie give up her milk, which she did without a protest. Everything we ate wit' was plastic; they gave us a plastic spork, tha bowl holdin' eggs was Styrofoam along wit' paper plate. Once done and they came to collect our trash a spork was missin'. It was obvious it was Sophie, who they dragged out kickin' and screamin'. Hannah sat tremblin' while I had to give ole gurl props for havin' tha courage to try. Hours later tha door opened and in strut this tall ass chick wit' a Mohawk. Hannah, always tha host, quickly introduced herself. "The names Sharon." she said wit' a thick ass accent. "Oh." gushed Hannah. "I love your accent, where are you from?" "The Bahamas, but I haven't been home in ages." said Sharon. Sharon was a'ight if you like 'em tall. She was definitely curvy and had sultry grey eyes. "And what's your name?" Before I could answer, Hannah replied, "That's Tay'. She was here before any of us." "For the record sweetie, I asked Tay'. She can talk right?" I smiled. Ooo, I like dis tall bitch. "Sorry." Of course you are boo; and if yo ass don't toughen us, yo ass ain't gonna surive. Sophie returned some time durin' tha night, wakin' everybody wit' her damn cryin'. "Oh my gosh!" I yelled. "Enough of tha cryin', did they break yo arm? Shove a broom up yo ass and you carryin' 'round a bunch of damn splinters? No, so shut tha hell up before I give you a reason!" "Thank you!" said Sharon. "Finally someone who sees shit my way." "They..they beat me." Sniff, sniff. "Then raped me." Sharon burst out laughin'. "Is that all? Girl shut up and grow a backbone." Now I laughed. "Ump I was thinkin' tha exact same thing." "Shut up!" Sophie screamed. "I was a virgin and they raped me! How can you p..women laugh at that?!" Ole Sophie sounds like she's on goin' Crazy Lane headed for Nervous

Break Down Avenue. Smirk. Sharon snorted. "All I know is I'm tryin to sleep. So suck that shit up, dry yo snotty face and go to damn sleep. Last warning chica." Growled Sharon. Sophie did as ordered; but not before crossin' tha room and climbin' in bed wit' Hannah. Hygiene taken care of, we trudged back to our room to find two more chicks sittin' atop beds; one white, one black and both looked like they'd been on the loosin' end of a brawl. I sniffed. Sharon frowned and snarled, "Who smells like Chicken of the Sea on wheat toast?" Neither girl said a word. "I know you ugly hoes heard me." The black girl who was well beyond black spat a "Fuck you." while the white girl kept her eyes low. Sharon smiled. "Maybe later once you scrub yo snatch homie, cause you foul." Yess! Serve her fishy ass a side of tartar sauce and fries boo! "So what are your names?" Asked Hannah tryin' a break the tension. "I'm Rochelle." said dark meat. "And that's Linda." "I heard more girls across the hall. I tripped on purpose and got a quick look inside before they dragged us in here." mumbled Linda. All eyes turned on her. "And?" I said promptin' dis chick to open her trap and spill it. "Well there were at least six beds and all of 'em looked full. A short black guy was givin' 'em the house rules, something about opening day and what's expected." "And?" Said Sharon. Linda shrugged. "That's it, that's all I heard." We all eyed each other. "Do you think we'll get the same speech?" questioned a wide eyed

Hannah. "Does yo face turn red when upset?" I snapped. "Hell yeah we're gonna hear tha speech. We'll be expected to fuck n suck fo' a buck. This is a hoe house and we are tha hoes. Damn, whatchu need, a house to fall on yo ass? This ain't Kansas boo and it ain't Oz either." Damn it felt good to let that shit out. The door swung open and in walked Larry Love who looked a lil taller. My eyes dropped, he had on black construction boots. Ump, don't catch a nosebleed boo. I'm just sayin'. Starin' right at me he gave a sickly grin. Nucca please. Yo short, stalkin' ass ain't doin' nothin' over here boo. Hell, you doin' me a favor okay; cause a bitch needed a break from Brandon and Joshua's mental asses, so try again. Shit didn't you know, Taylor loves tha dick boo. I need all the essential minerals and vitamins, I'm just sayin'. I blew Larry a kiss, his eyes widened. Ha! Sucka for tha nookie ass nigga! "A'ight listen up! Our employer has graciously deemed you lucky ladies the chance to turn yo lives around. You've been selected to work here to pleasure men and women if they so desire. You'll have more freedom once we see we can trust you." Larry stopped, then glanced at each girl before again starin' at me. What nucca, you want me to flash you a boob? Damn talk already, 'cause you gone make tha switch flip, okay. "Uh..yeah. So the more money you pull in, the more your stock rises, which in turn earns you certain perks. There's no way to escape. All doors and windows are secured and there'll always be security around. No ones lookin' for you, so get that thought outta yo heads. Any questions?" All hands went up. "Yeah the red head, sup?" Hannah nervously smiled. "Do we get to go outside once we earn perks?" "Fuck all that." cut in Sharon. "Do we get a cut for layin' on our backs and havin' sore jaws?" "Are we expected to fuck clients in this room?" Linda threw in. The questions kept comin' until exasperated, Larry yelled out, "shut up! Damn, do any of ya'll bitches have common sense?" He spat, muscle twitching in his jaw. "No you won't be allowed out. There's nothin' for miles but what you see now, trees. No you don't get a cut, fuck you think this is. No you won't fuck clients in here, this is ya'll sleepin quarters." Larry went in his pocket and pulled out slips of paper. "Everybody gets a number, remember it. Someone will take ya'll one by one to get gussied up and have yo pic taken for our customers to see their choices. Once trust is earned and you can move about freely, you'll all meet in the lobby once we open." With a last look my way, Larry knocked twice on tha door, walked out, leavin' us to our thoughts. True to Larry's word, one by one we were called out by our numbers, led down a hall blind folded and into a room where a rack of skimpy gear hung; and a small oval table sat with make-up and mirror, another table held all kinds of heels. I was lucky enough to get number six, so I didn't have to sit twiddlin' my thumbs, I needed a look-see on the layout. So far everythin' had been on tha first floor, so I started countin' tha steps it took to get from A to B. I knew they wouldn't keep us blind folded forever; so if trust was what they needed, I'd serve 'em up a big dose of it. Once I got away, these mafuckas better leave tha U.S. cause all bets were off. * Dove sipped a glass of wine, feeling relaxed in a tub full of hot bubbly water scented with jasmine oils. A soapy foot traveled up her leg. "How you feelin' ma?" Asked Kione who sat at the opposite end. She smiled. "Good bae. Thanks for the bath, it was a nice surprise." cooed Dove, batting her eyes. Kione smiled, "C'mon let's rinse off, your massage awaits." Smiling bright, Dove did as requested; then strode into the hotel room Kione had surprised her with. "Lay down." Kione huskily said, penis standing at attention. Smile bright, Dove stretched out face down then moaned when warm liquid was poured on her back and he slowly massaged; the smell of blueberries teased her nose. "Umm, that feels so good." said Dove, damn near droolin' she was so relaxed. Kione's hands lowered, gently rubbin' and squeezin' cheeks, then slowly lowered to backs of thighs; her legs splayed open offering up a slice of heaven. Kione didn't take the bait, instead he nibbled on her earlobe and whispered, "Turn over." Nipples hard, pussy soaked, Dove rolled over and opened her mouth wide; only for a slice of strawberry to be set on her tongue. 'Okay.' thought Dove. 'Not what I was expectin', but it's a start.' Kione continued massagin' while slidin' Dove pieces of cantaloupe, watermelon and cherries. "Feelin' better now?" Dove pouted. "A lil." Kione held up an L. "Well lets keeps the party goin'." And they did, ending it with a roundin' romp of toe curlin' sex and then drifted off to sleep. Frownin' at her reflection in tha bathrooms mirror, Dove stuck her tongue out. Kione still slept, so she tried not to let her anger escalate to where she destroyed the hotels bathroom. Things were goin' so good..and then Brian and his bullshit ruined it. Her eyes hardened wit' hate. She knew Tiphanie's ole rotten womb ass put Brian up to havin' her served wit' court papers. They were plannin' on takin' Jeff away from her. Why couldn't mafuckas leave her be? Her hands unconsciously squeezed the towel rack she'd been unaware of holdin' until she snatched it from the wall. The towel slid to the floor as Dove raised it to bash the mirror, then remembered Kione was in the bed. A small grin formed, Kione. Her smile widened becomin' more sadistic. Yess, Kione. So desperate, so eager to please.

CHAPTER FOUR

"**Y**ou!" Yelled one of the guards who still hid their identity behind masks. He then pointed at Hannah, "Come with me." Hannah nervously glanced around tha room, panic shinin' from her eyes. "Now!" He ordered. Skittish, heart poundin', Hannah sped across tha room and was quickly ushered out. "What was that about?" Linda asked. "Who cares." grunted Sharon, turnin' her hand this way and that as she painted her fingernails. Ump! Honestly, I'm glad Snow White got booted; 'cause she was on my last damn nerve, okay. Twenty-four seven her ass acted like she lived in a cave and ain't know shit 'bout tha world. I'm like, cut it out boo; cause every night you and Sophie bed hoppin', bumpin' and eatin' each other's pus' like we don't hear ya moanin' and meowin' when you buss a fat one, okay. Yo ass probably done slobbed on and rode more dicks then me okay, I'm just sayin'. Chatter was goin' back and forth when tha door opened and some heavy set mixed breed hoe wearin' a nightgown was shoved in tha room. Ole gurl looked like they kicked her ass real good, ya heard. She was willie lumped tha fuck up! Between tha bruises, tears and snot, I couldn't tell how she normally looked. "Damn gurl, who beat cho ass?!" I asked. Shit, maybe she ain't see it comin'. Yeah right. Chuckle. "Oh Lord, another crier." lamented Sharon with an eyeroll. Linda, havin' pity on snotty lump lump, helped her up and walked her over to Hannah's bed. Usin' lumpy's sleeve, Linda wiped her eyes and nose; and felt bad for whoever she was. A black and blue knot rested on her forehead, another covered her left cheek and one eye was swollen shut; even her lips were discolored. "It's okay, pull yourself together. You don't want them to hear you and they come back in here." Those words worked, 'cause she quickly cut that shit short. Thank God, 'cause a headache was loomin'. "You're right, thank you." a soft, wavery voice said. Linda patted her back, "What's your name?" she asked. "Tiphanie." Oh shit! My eyes widened. Ain't to many chicks stridin' round wit' tha name Tiphanie. I never got a look at her, but I knew she and Dove's brother/baby daddy were a couple. Ump, chile Dove's ass done flipped tha fuck out. A light clicked on. Dove! Ooo dat loony tunes behind all dis shit! That's why her ass wasn't home when Glenda and I got to her place. Tha shit was staged, she knew if we hadn't seen nor heard from her sooner or later we'd swing by. Anger raced through me. Dat jealous, hatin', back stabbin', loose pussy hoe! She ain't have half a brain to put dis into affect. So who was helpin' her besides Larry and Reba? I sneered, cause those two were non fuckin' factors. Dozens of possibilities came and went, 'cause not too many niggas stick around after taggin' Dove's wide load. Trust and believe, Taylor Janae James will figure it out; and God help 'em when I do. Grand opening had arrived. Dove made sure word got out about the opening and was ready to get shit poppin'. All the girls had a spin and knew what was what; and the punishment dealt out if they didn't comply. Dove smiled. Ole Taylor hadn't been a problem like she'd thought she'd be. She'd so looked forward to torturing her ass if she didn't do as told; but once again like a cat, the bitch landed on her feet. Dove lit up a cigarette contemplating her next move now that Tiphanie had joined the Dark Cavern stable. Just thinkin' about how she snatched Tiphanie got her pussy to jumpin'. Dove, Larry and Kione had cased out Brian and Tiphanie's house for three days, then made their move. Brian had enrolled Jeff in a daycare called Babies Like Us until his birthday when he'd attend Jamoke's pre-k class. That pissed

Dove off. 'How dare that barren bitch decide to put her son in daycare without askin' her input?' thought Dove. Brian had left for work, which angered her even more. 'Brian hadn't worked a day when we were together.' she stewed. The group waited an additional five minutes to make sure Brian didn't double back. Once the coast was clear, Dove told Larry and Kione to stand on the side of the house and once the door was open she'd signal them to join her inside. The plan worked beautifully. Upon seein' her knockin' through a curtain hung over the doors window, Tiphanie rolled her eyes, then yanked the door open; only to be shoved so hard she tripped over a garbage bag and fell on her ass. Larry and Kione fell in step behind her, then closed and locked the door. "Hi Tip', how's it goin'?" Dove had asked, even though her answer didn't matter. Stunned, eyes wide, Tiphanie stared between the three, pupils full of questions. "Stand up, we're gonna take a lil ride." Tiphanie's head rapidly shook in the negative. "No! Leave my house right this instant or I'll call the police!" Tiphanie had yelled in outrage. Dove gave a deep laugh. "Nah, you won't be callin' anyone. Boys, help ole Tiphanie up." Mouth open to scream, it was quickly shoved back down her throat when Larry tightly slapped his hand over it. Tiphanie bit the fleshy part of Larry's thumb, then prayed her jaw wasn't dislocated or worse; broken when a fist crashed into it. Her head smacked linoleum as both Kione and Larry rained punches everywhere. The last thing she saw before slippin' into dream land was Dove advancing, unfurling rope she pulled from her purse. Dove tweaked hardened nipples as she recalled Tiphanie's beatin' followed by Larry and Kione havin' a turn between cellulite thighs; her cell set on record catching every second. "Can I help you with that?" jarred Dove from thoughts of Tiphanie's kidnap, beating and rape. Hex, fresh from the shower, towel wrapped around his waist, beads of water cascadin' down muscular chest; had Dove comin' out of clothes lickety split. She sunk to her knees, yanked towel away and gently cupped Hex's sac. No more masks was my first thought when tha door swung open; and my damn mouth slid open when YoYo's jailbird ass strode all cocky like in tha room. Well I'll be a monkey's fuckin' uncle. YoYo and Reba were down wit' dis mess. Ooo I can't wait to take it to these he-she's! Okay, I mean buss they shit to tha white meat, red gravy baby! Seein' these two reassured me that I was dead on the money when I said Dove was behind alla this. I still hadn't seen Glenda who I hoped was alright 'cause Glenda had done nothin' but try to be dis loony bitches friend. Ump, some tricks just neva learn. They always twist shit to suit their wants and needs and have a fuckin' fit when shit doesn't go their way; ruinin' true friendships, fuckin' yo man behind yo back while smilin' in yo face, just skraight up triflin'. This hoe can never be me, no matter how bad she wants it. Why? 'Cause I keep shit real boo, I tell it like it mafuckin' is okay; and I don't give a hoot who don't like it, cause it's a free gotdamn country, just faker than a four dollar bill. I'm just sayin'. "Let's go." broke me from my thoughts. The six of us stood and followed behind them; gotta turn to pussy cause tha dick don't want cha ass bitches. I'll say one thing, walkin' around without a damn blindfold feels gooder then a mug. My eyes were bouncin' all over tha place. An emergency exit we passed was chained and padlocked, there were no windows, just a bunch of closed doors. Turnin' tha corner, my eyes widened. Thick black and grey carpet, cream colored alligator leather side tables, two chaise lounges and Italian lacquered baroque sofas. ump, Dove's ass ain't do this, her ass left her apartment lookin' like she was related to Billy goats, I'm just sayin'. Okay, 'cause any and errbody knows if yo bra and panties don't match and smell like Munster, yo apartment is definitely nasty boo okay. Anyhoo, on tha walls were big colored pictures of each girl dressed and lookin' fly; layin, sittin' wit' legs splayed. Eyes scannin' fo' Glenda's picture was halted as six more girls entered tha room and there she was. Glenda smiled, gave a nod and mouthed what looked like 'Dove'. Smirk. I know boo, and when I see dat tramp

they betta have my ass chained and surrounded, cause it's on!
"A'ight, show time ladies. Remember yo number, 'cause when
it's called you'll go down the opposite hall and use tha room that
corresponds with yo number." Barked Reba's ole pussy lickin'
behind. In walked a bunch of men. Ump a gotdamn smorgasbord;
tall, short, thin, hefty, black, white, Hispanic and more. When
they saw us positioned around tha room, eyes lit up and chops
were licked in anticipation. Girls were bein' picked left and right,
but we had no way of knowin' who picked us 'cause they were
told to pick tha number attached to tha bottom of tha frame.
"Number six." Aww shit, here we go, Standin', I strode towards
tha hall, frownin; when YoYo fell in step behind me. Damn hoe,
I don't need a fuckin' babysitter, just to walk a hall fulla
numbered doors okay. Yo ass must wanna watch; ole nasty,
crunchy boxers bitch. Too bad I don't got a broomstick to make
you feel at home, I'm just sayin'. Room six was filled wit'
everythin' a hoe needs to please tha custie; shit like eatable
underwear, fruits, whipped cream and whatnot. A glass cabinet
stood against tha wall that held whips, chains, cuffs, anal beads
and such; and was locked wit' a padlock. Tha door opened,
haltin' my perusal. Some tall, reed thin, hick complete wit'
cowboy boots and hat sauntered in like his ass was home range
bound, 'bout to fry up a freshly caught deer or some shit.

"Howdy lil lady. My my you sure are a pretty filly." Tha fuck is a filly? Country boy gone get a chop to tha throat if dats slang for nigga. "Hmm, well hello stranger. What's yo pleasure this evenin'?" Gag. He smiled, revealin' three of his bottom choppers were missin'. Maybe that filly knocked them joints out, I'm just sayin'. "Aww shucks ma'am, well, to be honest this is my first time in this type of establishment. Plus I've never laid wit' a colored female before, so I'm kinda nervous. Maybe you can take the reins on this one." Chile, I ain't understand half tha shit country boy said, my ass still tryina decipher what tha hell a filly is okay. They should have a 'how to understand country boys' for dummies up in here boo, okay. Smile wide, I crossed tha room. Stoppin' right in front of him, I ran a hand from tha top button on his shirt to his belt buckle, which by tha way was big as hell and had a pic of horse and rider on it. "First timer eh? A'ight, just relax and let dis filly fulfill all yo desires." "Uhm, okay. My names Billy Ray by the way." Yawn. Ninja I don't give a good gotdamn what cho name is, unless its first name: Will Help last: You Escape okay boo. So don't tell me yo life story, 'cause yo ass will put me in a damn coma. Billy Bob, Billy Goat, what tha hell never nodded, then swallowed. His Adams apple bobbed all kinds of crazy in a chicken neck he called a throat. Unbuttonin' his flannel shirt brought into view a patch of hair on a ribs and protrudin' chest; and when pants and boxers dropped, good googily moogily. Dis ninja was scrawny as hell! Just extra damn bony. I know when he walked and dem bones shook and rattled he looked and sounded crazy. Ump, so damn skinny his nipples touch; so skinny ass and balls look like one item; so skinny he looks like a mic stand, I'm just sayin'. Seven curved inches was surrounded by patches of pubic hair. Da fuck ninja, you got alopecia of tha balls? I'd already swiped a condom, so I tore it open, placed it in my mouth and sucked him in. "Sshit!" squealed out as his toes balled up in knots. Well damn boo, I ain't even get started yet and yo ass already 'bout to blow. Smirk, cause dats what happens when you come to tha best boo okay, you get hooked a'ight. You start missin' work so you can be first in line when tha doors open; eyes peeled lookin' fo' me okay. I'm just sayin'. "Cats whiskers, please don't stop!" He pleadingly yelled, hips pistonin'. Breathe okay, cause CPR is extra ninja. Something thumped on tha floor. Gazin' downward, I see ole Billy Bob's cell done fell out his pocket. Alright now! Easin' up a lil, 'cause now I don't want his ass comin' jack rabbit quick. I reached down, flipped it open and didn't see a lock code. Damn what's Ty's number? Or Omaire for that matter? Fuckin' A B and C! Think Tay', think! All I could remember of Omaire's number was the first three and the last four of Ty's. Ooo, I could beat my own ass right now! Flippin' tha phone closed, I took care of Billy Jean, then got ready for tha next customer. Six custies later I was mad as fuck. I'm like how I'm a hoe in a hoe house givin' up tha pus' fo' free and not nan one got me off or had a fuckin' cell that wasn't locked. Kinda shit is that!? It's like havin' fifty cents to use a payphone and not ones in sight cause SNET (Southern New England Telephone) done pulled 'em all up. Not everybody has a cell phone okay and even if they do, half tha time yo joints off cause you ain't pay tha bill. It's like yo rag startin' and ain't a pad or tampon in sight, I'm just sayin'. Anyhoo, I did clip a few dollars from each custie though. Twenty from Billy Goat, the last outta some dude who said his name was Jones; cheap bastard only had five bucks. Anotha had nothin' but lint; wallet so dry moths flew out, I'm just sayin'. I stuck it inside tha kitty kat bank in case they wanna strip search a bitch. Surprisingly we all were allowed to shower before bein' escorted back to our prison. The next day, peppermint breath came and drug Tiphanie kickin' and screamin' from tha room. "Sup wit' that?" Rochelle asked; which shocked me 'cause I thought tha hoe was mute or somethin'. "What?" asked Sharon, eyin' Rochelle all hard. "Why they take ole girl? She came back later then us and now she's out before breakfast's even served. Let me find out she's the favorite, she'll start snitchin' on all of us." A few brows arched at Rochelle's words. "Nah it ain't that." threw out Linda, "Last night before they came for us, she started tellin' me that some chick name Dove beat her up and took her from her home. Said dis Dove chicks gotta buncha loose screw that she's angry and bitter cause her baby daddy took her kid and wants nothin' to do wit' her." Yeah, yeah, tell it to tha choir. Betta yet, tell me somethin' I don't fuckin' know, okay boo. If you gone spread tha news at least get somethin' I ain't heard or figured out my damn self, I'm just sayin'. No one said a word, I guess to let her words marinate. Anyhoo lunch of hotdogs, French fries and grape Kool-Aid that tasted like it ain't have a drop of sugar came in. I'm sayin', Kool-Aid's a hood staple okay. How you gone make some and leave out tha damn sugar? That's like yo pus' fallin' off and you still tryin to fuck. It's like wantin' yo dick sucked but no one will touch it cause its fulla big ass pus bumps, okay. Disgusted, I left that shit and just ate tha lunch that was in-between lukewarm and cold. Chatter between tha girls went back and forth, which I pretty much ignored til talk turned to tha guards. "I heard that afro wearin' dyke lookin' chicks pretty dangerous." said one. Another sucked her choppers and spat, "I heard she's been in and out of jail a rack of times." "So fuckin' what!" snapped Rochelle. "People go to jail every damn day, that shit means nothin'." "True. said Sharon, joinin' in. "I found out that Reba chicks really a dude." Jaws hung open at her words. "Oh yeah, how you figure?" I asked. Fuck it, I joined in; ain't like I got shit else to do. "The other day when she walked me to the bathroom, I lied and said there wasn't no toilet paper. So when she got some and handed it over, I accidently ran my hand over crotch and was about to offer a pussy lick when I ain't feel no pussy. In other words, Reba ain't no damn chick, she's a dude." "No way!" "Get outta here!" "You lie!" Were all tossed out when Sharon shared that juicy tidbit of news. Ump, yes boo. Ron, Reba, whateva tha fuck she's callin' herself this month was definitely not a male; 'cause dick wasn't swingin' between her thighs unless she had on a strap on, I'm just sayin'. Tha door swung open and Tiphanie's shoved back in tha room. All talk ceased 'cause ole Tiphanie looked zoned tha hell out. Before I knew it, I'd crossed tha room and stood before Tiphanie. Her head bobbed around on her neck, along wit' eyes that continually rolled in their sockets. "Tip." I smacked her ass. "Focus. What happened?" "Hunh?" A lil drool ran from lip to chin. Gross ass. I gave a lil shake. "What'd they do to you Tip'?" I asked again cause a bitch needed to know if they planned on doin' to me what they'd done to her ass. Fuck everyone else, this was all about self preservation ya heard. "I..uh.." her voice faded out and tha head bob started back up. Linda burst out laughin'.

"Fuck so funny?" Snarled Rochelle, chile all this cattiness was givin' my ass a headache, okay. "The bitch is high; most likely heroin. Trust, I know the signs when I see 'em." Aww shit, ugly girls right. Bitch so ugly her name should be 'shit happens'. She so ugly her Doctor is a vet, I'm just sayin'. Damn, her ugly ass got me off track. What was I sayin'? Oh yeah, Tiphanie was higher than a kite. Snatchin' both arms I gave 'em a look-see and sure 'nough, a needle prick lay in crook of her arm. Damn, Dove has truly gone too damn far okay; just totally done lost it boo, skraight coo cook for coco puffs. I'm sayin', has this chick always been crazy and just hid it when around my ass? I swear I ignored all signs, figurin' Dove was just jealous when all along tha hoe was plottin' and schemin'. Fuck!

THE END

ABOUT
THE AUTHOR

New York Times & International Best Selling Author Billie
Dureyea Shell was born in Compton California and now lives
in Ladera Heights with his wife and
kids who he loves to spend time with.
He is the Owner of several properties in the Los Angeles area
and gives back to his community by providing low income
housing to those who need it.
He stated "It doesn't matter where you at or where you from
it's what you do with your time. There's nothing you can't do
if you put your mind to it".